JUSTICE

JUSTICE

Emerald Trilogy:
Book 3

QUINN MINNICH

Anya Minnich

Quinn Minnich

Contents

1   The Dragon Tracker   1

2   Help from the Desert   20

3   Travels   37

4   Sorrow's Pity   57

5   The Dragon Trainer   79

6   The Final Night   101

7   Dragon Rider   122

Epilogue   152

I

The Dragon Tracker

Through the forests of the Shadowlands, a figure on horseback galloped at full speed for the north. The horse, bred for speed and stamina, was panting with exhaustion after three days of hard travel. The rider was Justice. For three mornings, three evenings, and three nights he had sped on at a relentless pace, pausing only for a few hours at a time to give his mount a rest. Wherever he went—in every village and town he passed— he always asked the same question: *Where could he find the emerald dragon?* They would point to the skies, tell the direction where the creature had last been seen, name the area or town it had been headed toward, and Justice would immediately set out again in hard pursuit. None refused him; none challenged him. There was something in the man's eyes that warned against opposition.

On and on Justice rode. He had ridden for days but still his eyes were focused, his mind alert. He was coming in for the kill. Recently he had been getting closer; the distance between him and his target had been shrinking. That morning he had even seen a glimpse of the dragon in

the skies, fleeing before him; now he saw it land in a clearing up ahead. Whether to rest or wait for him he did not know, but Justice rode all the harder. Anger boiled through him—hatred toward the dragon that had murdered his brother and for the man who controlled it.

He felt the Link around his neck bounce against his chest as the horse continued to gallop forward. It gave him glimpses, just hints, of the fleeing dragon's thoughts, which gave him the information necessary to track it even when there was no one to ask. Justice was determined and relentless—any other soldier would have given up the chase by now, but not him. Justice could not be stopped, bribed, or opposed; he would ensure that the man paid for what he had done, if it was the last thing he did.

The sun had passed its peak in the sky when he slowed his horse to a halt. He carefully dismounted, placing the saddle bag he carried with him around his shoulder, and rested his hand briefly on his panting mount. It had carried him far, but now it could rest. Now he would proceed alone.

He advanced forward through the trees and into a large clearing. On three sides the open space was surrounded by forest, and on the fourth a large river blocked further passage north. In the center of the clearing stood the dragon Ember, and upon his back was seated the man—Deception.

"Welcome Justice, my relentless pursuer," he jeered from his mount. "Have you finally come to meet your death?"

Justice halted and let his saddle bag drop to the ground. He rested a hand on his katana. "You must be getting desperate to have stopped to face me," he said.

Deception laughed, though a little nervously. "You have great faith in your abilities," he said. "I still have no idea what you did in Despair or to Ruthless, but even you have your limits. You yourself know the power of the Dragon Rider; you grew up with it in your own country. How can you possibly hope to challenge me and my dragon?"

"That dragon is not yours, and you are not the Dragon Rider. Get down off your stolen mount and face me like a man!"

Deception smiled and drew his saber. Ember growled.

"Why don't you come over here and force me?"

"I will."

"Ha! I'd like to see you try; even you cannot hope to defeat me. Today I will be rid of your pestilence!"

"I'm telling you for the last time," said Justice, his voice low. "Get down from him."

Deception snarled. "Make me!"

The air rang with the sound of steel as Justice drew his sword, and in response Ember leapt into the air, his wings beating powerfully until he had risen twenty feet off the ground. He stopped there, hovering above the clearing, well out of reach.

"All right, Justice, miracle worker!" hollered Deception. "Do the impossible again if you can! But this time you will die!"

And as if in agreement, Ember roared and blasted fire down.

With no other choice, Justice ran as the ground exploded in flame. He had been determined to find Deception, but had not known what to expect when the battle finally came. Now, with no plan and the dragon too high up to reach, he did the only logical thing he could, which was to run directly underneath Ember and hide in his shadow. Above he heard the beast roar and growl as it twisted and turned in midair, but it seemed unable to look directly beneath itself without diving, and so the flame it madly rained down fell wide of its target.

Justice considered holding his position and letting the dragon drain itself of fire, which would happen eventually, but he knew that he would not be able to stay underneath the beast forever. Soon, Ember began to counter his strategy by suddenly darting away in random directions, hoping to catch his target out in the open. But Justice was fast! He could feel through the Link which direction Ember planned to go and was always able to stay under him, dashing along the ground and leaping over fire that smoldered in the grass. Each time, however, the dragon flew faster and farther, and each time Justice found himself dodging more and more flame as the landscape became more charred.

But through the Link, Justice knew that Ember was becoming increasingly frustrated, and so finally, when the dragon darted yet again, Justice turned the opposite way and ran out from under its shadow. He guessed that he would have around eight seconds before the dragon turned around, realized what had happened, and destroyed him while he was out in the open. He began to count down in his mind.

Eight, seven...

He felt Ember preparing to turn, but kept his eyes on the ground ahead.

...six, five...

Up ahead lay the forest, but he would not have time to reach it. He felt Ember turn.

...four, three...

Ember seemed confused, but then spotted him and roared. Justice kept running.

...two, one!

At the last moment, Justice spun around at full speed to see the dragon up in the sky above him, fire forming in its throat.

"I said *come down!*" he roared, and with all the momentum of his turn he hurled his katana up toward the dragon.

***

Deception saw it coming. He watched as if in slow motion as the glimmering blade came spinning toward them, arcing slightly in its path as all curved things do, and as it slashed directly through Ember's left wing.

With a screech that shook the earth, Ember tilted in his flight and the fire got caught in his throat. Desperately Deception tried to regain control, but the pain that pulsed through Ember, like fire with every beat of his wing, was more than he could bear. Still bellowing in agony, the dragon leaned dangerously to the left, lost his balance, and began tumbling and spinning toward the ground. Deception tried to pull him back but only succeeded in getting him to level out moments before hitting the earth. They struck with such force that Ember's body plowed a short trench through the dirt before coming to a halt.

The dragon groaned a low, moaning sound, but then let its head fall against the grass. Deception picked himself up and looked forward, trying to get his bearings.

Justice was coming toward him!

With a bolt of horror, Deception sat up and shook his downed dragon by the horns. "Get up! Get up!" he hissed.

Ember groaned slightly but otherwise did not respond. Deception looked up. Before them marched Justice, calmly, resolutely, and with an air of finality. Smoothly Justice drew his dagger as he approached, his cloak billowing slightly in the wind behind him. Deception tried frantically to get Ember to rise again, but without success.

"Fight me like a man!"

With terror Deception looked up and struggled to get his saber raised. Before him, Justice leapt onto Ember's snout, pulled himself up by a horn, and brought his dagger down just as Deception managed to raise his own weapon to block. The blades met with a resounding crash and Justice pulled himself up onto Ember's head, pushing Deception back.

For the next few moments the two of them fought bitterly in the confined space upon the slippery scales; Justice was clearly at an advantage however, as he had the smaller weapon. Many times, Deception found his saber too long and awkward to properly block or stab at such close quarters, and his assailant fought with a grim, measured air of determination and anger. Finally, Deception's desperation grew so great that he risked a duck under the sweep of the dagger and rammed into his opponent, wrapping his arms around his waist and knocking them both off the dragon's neck and onto the grass.

Instantly Justice was on his feet and at Deception once again, but now his dagger, a blessing before, was proving a deadly disadvantage out in the open. Deception was a skilled fighter and with each sweep of his saber he forced his opponent back. Justice tried to edge around his assailant back toward Ember, but Deception was not about to let his dragon be taken, not by any means. Again and again he struck out, and again and again Justice was forced farther back, his opponent becoming more confident and more fierce with every moment.

Then, just as they neared the tree line, Deception broke through with his sword and cut a small gash upon Justice's left arm as he leaped to the side. He watched Justice fall to the ground, do a roll, and then spring back up again, his dagger in one hand and his bloodied katana in the other.

Suddenly Deception realized that he had been outwitted. From the moment Ember was struck Justice had noted where his sword fell and had been edging toward it the entire time. Now, as Deception lunged at him, hacking wildly, Justice was able to easily block, duck, and strike out, forcing Deception back.

Now the battle had reached its final turn. Deception battled as fiercely and as wildly as he could, but though he may have been able to best his opponent while he held the longer blade, he did not stand a chance against the feared general while he wielded both his weapons.

Viciously they fought back across the smoldering grass, edging closer to the forest trees. Deception felt a fear unlike any he had ever experienced as he battled his doom, his nightmare, the man who could not be stopped by armies or castles or dragons. Justice fought with a cold determination; his blades flashed like lightening as he spun and blocked and ducked and leapt with the agility and grace of a dancer. His blades seemed to be everywhere at once.

Then, without warning, Justice hurled his dagger as he spun, and sent it whirling through the air, grazing Deception's right hand and imbedding itself into a tree trunk beyond. With a cry Deception nearly dropped his saber as he attempted to grasp it with both hands. Justice gripped his katana with both hands as well and began to beat upon his opponent's upraised sword with tremendous strength.

"For Highland!" he cried, and Deception was forced back against the trees as he desperately tried to hold out against the assault.

"For my brother!"

Deception stumbled and fell, his saber still blocking as his grip weakened.

"For the King!"

With a final cry, Justice spun his katana around in a full circle and knocked Deception's saber clear out of his hands and across the grass. His opponent tried to roll to the side, but Justice was quicker and leaped upon him, landing on his chest and holding the blade to his throat.

"Now you will die!"

Deception scowled back.

"If I'm to die, then at least I lived to see the day when the Justice of Highland became corrupted."

"What are you talking about?" Justice demanded, his katana ready to strike.

"Tell me: is it justice if you kill out of revenge? Admit it. You're not here to fulfill the law—you're being led by your own fury!"

Justice growled louder. "I made a promise to my brother."

"A promise?" said Deception, confused. "What type of promise? I find it unlikely that his dying wish would have been for you to kill..." His eyes settled on the form of Ember beyond them, who was shaking his head and beginning to get up. Deception smiled and laughed heartily. "You?" he said turning back to Justice and grinning with disbelief. "You? Peace chose *you* to rescue his dragon, to be the *Dragon Rider*?" He laughed again, even louder.

Justice's expression darkened. "Yes, he has; and now I that have freed the dragon from you, it is time for your death."

"Ah, but if given the choice, would you kill me or save Ember? Would you rather honor your brother, or avenge him?"

Justice's voice was cold. "I would follow my brother's last wish."

Deception's eyes narrowed. "Then prove to me that you are ruled by a higher motive than revenge!"

And with lightning speed he drew a hunting blade with one hand to counter Justice's katana, and with the other sounded a small red horn.

Instantly, behind them, Ember screeched and leaped up in fear. He stumbled, fluttered uselessly on his injured wing, and fell into the river where he floundered, trying to stay afloat. Justice turned to look—just for a second—and Deception took that chance to throw him off, lunge for his saber, and leap to his feet. Justice immediately turned to face him, but Deception was not staying to fight. Instead he turned and fled to Justice's horse standing at the edge of the clearing, mounted it, and sped off through the trees.

"Go ahead! Save him; ride him! See if you can last the week without killing the beast that murdered your brother!" he shouted over his shoulder. Then he was gone.

Slowly, Justice turned to the river. Ember had managed to flounder through the water to the other side and was pulling himself up onto dry land. He stumbled to his feet, shook his head with a whimper, and then lumbered clumsily forward into the trees, moaning and whining with fright.

Justice spat bitterly, stabbing his sword into the ground and pacing the clearing. Now what was he supposed to do? Just let Deception go? And rescue a condemned dragon that would need to die? He shook his head with rage but knew the only option. He had made a promise, and he never broke a promise.

Turning around, he marched over to the tree where his dagger protruded, pulled it out, and then collected his saddle bag from where it lay in the grass. Then with firm resolution he headed in the direction that Ember had gone and washed his weapons in the river—one stained with the blood of a man, the other with the blood of a dragon.

***

Deception shook his head angrily as he galloped away at a reckless pace. So, he had finally lost Ember. But all things considered, it was only an inconvenience. Did he fail to kill Justice? Yes. Had he wanted to keep the dragon? Of course! But the battle could have gone worse—he could have lost his life! Deception wondered at his continued good luck. First, he had survived the fall off a cliff, and now he had escaped Justice's sword. He would need to be more careful—his fortune might not hold out forever.

He turned the horse to the left and began to head upriver to where he knew there would be a bridge. It would take him awhile to cross and by then Justice and Ember could be anywhere, but it didn't matter now. His plan had been to destroy the Dragon Rider Pact, and he had succeeded with Peace's death. Ember was the only remaining member and Justice, while holding the legal right to him, would not be named his official Rider until they both stood before the King. Deception smiled. Justice might even do him a favor if he killed Ember before they reached the King; then the Pact would be destroyed for good and there would be no heir to take the throne. His victory would be complete!

However, losing Ember had not been part of his plan. But then again, his plan had not really extended this far. He wanted to be riding the beast when he battled the King—but he had plenty of other dragons. He did not need Ember to kill the King. In fact, he didn't really need Ember at all now. All that mattered was the final battle with the King— and it was even rumored that he would be coming here, playing right into his hands! And now Justice would likely be too occupied to inter- fere. Deception smiled. His revenge, his conquest, his victory was almost complete!

***

It had taken Justice a while to cross the river, but he had eventually managed to do it. He first threw his weapons and saddle bag across and then, by swimming out in a diagonal against the current, he made it to the other shore. Now, as he gathered up his things and set off to find Ember, the sun was starting to set and the light beginning to grow dim. It was by no means hard to follow the path of the dragon however. Apparently unable to fly on its injured wing, it had crashed a destructive path through the trees in no set direction.

Silently, Justice began to wonder what type of trouble Ember might get into as he roamed the woods alone, conflicted, and afraid. Had he been held prisoner by Deception so long that he would desperately submit to the first human he encountered? Would he even be capable of staying independent, or would the emptiness kill him? Then suddenly through the trees ahead, Justice began to hear a commotion that grew louder with each step he took. Placing his hand on his katana, he burst into a full run. He broke into a clearing and skidded to a stop in horror.

He had come across a small village, composed of what appeared to be a primitive tribe. The villagers were fleeing in every direction from the form of a great dragon in their midst—*Ember*. The beast seemed nearly as confused as the people, moaning and whimpering like an injured horse. Many of the tribe's straw huts were ablaze and villagers were laying along the ground screaming, crying, burnt, and injured. Several of the strongest warriors were attempting to fend off the dragon with spears, but Ember took no heed, apparently distracted by the emotional torrents inside of him. He wreaked destruction and panic with nearly every movement of his body.

Justice's eyes narrowed and his world grew dark. He had half-drawn his katana before barely managing to get a hold of himself. The rage inside him boiled. With fevered energy he drew forth Ember's Link from his saddle bag, ensured that the chain was unfastened, and then—clenching the pendant tightly in his hand—he charged the roaring dragon.

People passed by in a blur as he ran between blazing buildings. Ahead he watched as Ember swung his claw at the village soldiers and then reared back to blast fire. Justice quickly ducked as flame shot over his head and then he dove and rolled to the side, grabbing a fallen spear as he did so. He leaped to his feet and ran around the side of the enraged dragon, ducking a blind sweep of its tail. Quickly judging his angle, Justice made a charge for the dragon's flank and used his spear to vault himself up. He hit the scales of Ember's side hard, and just barely managed to catch one of the spikes that ran along the beast's back. Swiftly, he pulled himself up and ran toward the dragon's head. He swung the Link through the air at the end of its chain.

"Ember! Stop!" he cried, but the dragon didn't notice him. With a shout, Justice leaped forward, grabbed one of the dragon's horns, and swung the Link against the side of Ember's neck. Its momentum was enough to catch the scales and fling the pendent up and around the other side where Justice swiftly caught it. Hooking the two ends of the chain together, he let the Link fall into place and called out with both mind and voice: *Ember! Stop this now!*

The Link seemed to have no impact on Ember, so Justice, his rage and anger built up to their peak, gripped the scales of Ember's neck with all his might and hollered an indiscernible command.

His touch had an immediate effect.

Justice never really knew what he expected would happen when he touched Ember. Perhaps since Deception had produced hunger, it was logical to assume the same would happen again. Had he commanded a slightly calmer temper, he might have remembered that the emotion imparted would be strongly connected to one held foremost in his mind, but Justice did not remember and was therefore shocked when he felt the effect of his own hand.

It was pure fire.

Instantly Ember screeched in pain, a pain unlike any other he had ever felt. It burned him to the core; it seemed to blaze through every part of him, as though his soul had been ripped apart in the midst of a searing, scorching flame. He roared, he shook, he trembled, and through the deeps of his mind he called out a single word:

Please!

Justice had already stopped, mostly out of surprise than anything else, but then his anger returned and he laid hold of the dragon again, probing deeper into the fury of his mind. Beneath him, Ember cried out in even greater pain and agony. He shrieked and shook his head from side to side, but he soon grew too weak for that. He bellowed for mercy as fire coursed through his veins, but still Justice held on. Ember sank to his knees, the pain ravaging his soul and body.

Please! he called out. *Please, stop!*

Still Justice held on. He felt no pain or compassion for the creature he tortured, but it was not out of rage that he continued. He could feel the fire, as it ate deeper into Ember's mind, burn away everything else—the confusion, the loneliness, the hunger, even the effects of Deception's influence, seemed to melt away under the heated pressure.

Stop! I'll do anything! Who are you?

Justice leaned in close to the dragon's ear.

"Don't you remember me?" he whispered. "I'm Justice; the brother of the man you killed."

And then he released him. Instantly Ember felt the effect dissipate and fell prostrate to the ground, panting and trying to regain his breath. Justice felt the dragon's mind quickly revert to its former state of confusion and tangled emotions, though not quite to the degree it had been before.

There was a holler and then a cheer. Justice looked up to see a large band of the village people standing before him, raising spears in the air and shouting cries of amazement and triumph to their new-found savior. Justice quickly looked down at the back of Ember's head.

Ember! he called. *Get up! We have to go—now!*

The dragon did not respond. He was slowly regaining his feet, shaking his head. The cheers grew quieter. Justice grimaced and held his hand inches away from the dragon's scales, feeling the slight effect that even that had.

"I said to get up!" he threatened. "Get out of here now!"

Ember whimpered again at the threat of the man's fire and immediately turned, stumbling away through the woods as quickly as he could. Their journey however was awkward and difficult through the close trees and tangled underbrush.

"Why don't you fly?" asked Justice angrily.

I can't. My wing is injured—I've tried.

Justice grumbled but led the dragon through the trees a distance and over a stream before letting him halt in a clearing. The sun had nearly set.

"We can stop here," he said, dismounting.

Ember was silent and settled into a crouch as close to the trees as he could. Justice paid him little heed and went about gathering dry brush and kindling to make a fire. Both were silent for a long time, and it was Ember who finally broke the stillness.

Did you kill him?

"What?"

Is Deception still alive?

Justice looked up from the fire he had started and eyed Ember oddly.

"Yes, he got away."

Immediately he felt Ember's relief through the Link. Justice's eyes narrowed. "Is that all you care about? Not the village you just destroyed?"

Ember growled a deep rumbling sound. *I couldn't understand what was going on around me. I was confused and in pain—and that was thanks to you! I was happy with Deception; he gave me joy, purpose, love. And then you came along, slashed my wing, and tore me away! How did you think I would respond?*

"Do care *nothing* for your old Rider? For Peace? I thought you wanted him; I thought you loved him! Can't you at least the honor his memory by not taking the side against him?"

I did love him! roared Ember, nearly rising to his feet. *I loved him with all my heart; he was...he was everything I had...and when he died, I had nowhere left to go. I was in pain, agony; I needed comfort, safety, forgiveness and there was no one to turn to except Deception. I certainty couldn't have turned to you!*

Justice was on his feet, his eyes ablaze. "So you have no remorse at all! You killed your master, joined his enemy, and now scorn me, the one he sent to save you!"

Ember stood, growling threateningly. *Don't you dare judge me! You have no idea what I've been through, nor the pain I've endured!*

"Your pain is your own making! You are more despicable than all the criminals I have ever hunted down. I ought to run you through right now as the law demands!"

You think just because you hit me once that you can challenge me face-to-face? I'd like to see you try!

Justice roared in rage and drew his katana as Ember crouched low and readied his fire. The two stared at each other for several seconds, tensions high, waiting to see who would strike first.

Then Justice grunted and thrust his sword into the ground. "No!" he said. "I will not kill you now. I made a promise to take you first to the King. Then I will kill you."

Ember settled down, if only slightly. *If you will kill me anyway, then why should I let you take me anywhere?*

"Because I've made an attempt to rescue you and if you choose to leave me I can claim that you are beyond hope and I will be released from my promise. Trust me, if you go back to that accursed man again, I *will* hunt you down and kill you, just like the King will to every one of Deception's followers."

But if I'm to die either way, why should I choose to spend the last of my days with you? At least Deception didn't burn like fire whenever he touched me.

"Look, I tracked you down only because I promised to do so. As for your own part, you might want to consider redeeming your legacy. You're already the first dragon to ever kill its own Rider; the best you can do now is at least have people know you repented of it in the end. Or if you prefer, you can always be remembered as Deception's pet."

Ember backed off a little and lowered himself to the ground. *If you really are planning to save me, then why slay me at the end of it all?*

"Because the law demands it! You committed treason of the highest order! I am bound by the law to put you to death, whether or not I want to—though I admit that my feelings for you will by no means get in the way."

Treason? You call my killing of Peace treason? I was under a Curse! You think I wanted to do that? I had no choice!

"Oh, don't give me that!" Justice spat angrily. "Peace died with the Curse in his hand! You had the choice, did you not?"

Even detached from me it still—

"Did you?" Justice roared.

Ember glared hard at him, but then lowered his head. *Yes, I had the choice.*

"Then you are guilty of treason."

I had no other option! Peace told me to do it!

"Even if I believed that, how badly could you really have loved Peace? Tell me, did you wait even a full minute after you blasted my brother into oblivion before returning right back to your old slavery? How quickly did you run back to Deception—the one Peace *died* freeing you from? For how long did you willfully serve him before he ever placed you under the Curse? No, my friend, you are *saturated* with treason, there is no question about your guilt."

You think I wanted to kill Peace! Ember growled with rage. *He was my Rider! I loved him! Killing him tore me apart!*

"And you think that you were the only one who loved him?" Justice shouted. "I was there before you were born! For years I stood by his side as I watched him tending to you, caring for you, spending every spare moment with his little hatchling! He devoted every ounce of affection he had to you, but there were others who cared for him! His father, his people, his country—your murder tore him away from them all!"

Peace was everything to me! You have no idea what I lost!

"Oh, I know how much he loved you. He loved you so much that he died for you without a second thought as to how it would impact those who loved him. He loved you so much that his *dying wish* was for me to save you. He proclaimed me Rider without a thought as to what it would mean to Highland or Tarenthia. I could never be half the man my father is, and yet Peace considered nothing except for who would be most able to save *you*."

Ember tossed his head and made a snorting sound. *Well, I can agree with you on that point; you'd make a horrible Rider.*

"And you are a horrible dragon! Tell me, why have you not responded to anything I've said through the Link?"

You spoke to me through the Link?

"Yes, twice."

Interesting...though I'm certainly not surprised.

"Why do you say that? I can hear you just fine."

The Links are designed so that any human wearing one can listen to dragons. My Link however will only receive the thoughts of one who is part of the Dragon Rider Pact.

"I am part of the Pact! Peace made me so!"

Do you understand nothing about this? Legally yes, you hold the right to be the Rider, but the Pact can only be formed if both the Rider and dragon choose to be bonded to one another. I can tell by your simmering rage that you have not chosen me, and I can guarantee that I will never choose you!

Justice snarled and turned away. He was done speaking to a creature just as stubborn as himself. Mindlessly he stoked the fire and eventually Ember turned away and lay down, dozing off. Justice however could not sleep; he stayed up throughout the night, wondering what on earth he had gotten himself into and gazing periodically at the crescent moon in the sky.

2

Help from the Desert

Dawn was slowly breaking when Justice thought of his saddlebag. It held few things, but he still took his time searching through it in the dim light. Next to him the fire had died down into embers—small, broken embers that glowed faintly, a ghostly tale of the warmth and heat they used to give. Justice sighed. Why was he here? It was all wrong. He was never meant to be the Dragon Rider—he could easily admit that. It had always been Peace's special skill to love and promote life and prosperity. He could only produce judgment and death.

Justice looked down in his lap at the two letters he had found. The first, from his brother, was opened and named him as the next Rider. Justice put it to the side. The second was from the King.

While I hope you will never need to use this, I give this to you for the hour of greatest need. When you are at your wit's end, and when you cannot see how to go on, read this and I believe it will provide help.

Justice looked at the envelope grimly for a few moments and then broke the seal. If there was ever a time where all seemed impossible, it was now. By the dim light of the early morning he read his father's writing.

My dear son Justice,

I instructed you to only open this letter in your hour of greatest need, but I think we both know that if you faced war or impossible odds you would be searching for a way to overcome, rather than looking for help. The only way, in fact, that you could be driven to your wit's end would be if you faced something you felt yourself incapable of handling. Therefore, if you are reading this, then the worst I have feared has happened. Peace has been killed, and he has named you to be the Dragon Rider.

He had spoken to me of his plans before he left, and so I knew that it would be a possibility. I have no doubt you now feel as though no worse choice could be made, that while you would physically be able to fight for the dragon, you would be unable to care for him. But right now, you are exactly what Ember requires. Before Deception, he needed Peace; he thrived on the gentle love and care your brother provided. But now he has been corrupted, and gentle love can no longer pierce his pain and deception. It takes fire and punishment to break through that, and only you can provide it.

I once told you that dragons are prone to aggression and bravery, that having one of your own would only heighten your sense of justice. But Ember is different; he has been broken, he has seen the darkness within him and now his pride is shattered. I believe that if he could be brought back, he would make an even wiser dragon than all his predecessors. Bring him to me and take the chance to learn from him; I will ensure he receives his punishment in due time according to the law.

You are the Dragon Rider now, and I believe, even if you do not, that you are capable of this calling. Have faith and try; I would not call you to something you could not do. If you still feel however that you and Ember are incapable of working together, then as a final word of advice I suggest that you head into the desert which lies to the east. Having been there before, I know the lay of the

land and believe that the two of you may find help in that place. Whatever you choose however, make hast and hurry north to meet me. My mercy holds until the night of the full moon. Ensure you are with me by that time!

Godspeed, my son.

Justice looked up from the letter and let it fall to his lap. It was comforting to read the words of his father, but they did not appear to be much help. He still didn't know how to work with Ember, or how to be the Dragon Rider, and the only hope the letter seemed to offer at all was some mysterious help to the east which they hardly had the time for. The moon would be full in just under two weeks, and there was no telling how far north they had to travel.

Justice was suddenly distracted by a disturbance through his Link and looked up at Ember. The dragon was still asleep and appeared to be dreaming, his body twitching. Justice was able to catch glimpses of emotion through the Link; glimpses of fear, of pain, of loneliness, of...hunger!

Justice leapt to his feet. It was there, a very strong feeling that Ember associated with Deception's touch. He felt within the dragon's tortured mind the longing to feel it again, to be comforted by the sad yet ravenous desire for some unknown object, to give up control of himself to that man once again.

Justice quickly moved toward Ember to wake him, but was struck when he sensed an unexpected emotion in the dragon—guilt. Something within Ember resisted the longing; it did so weakly and feebly but it was there nonetheless, trying to pull back the rest of his mind from succumbing to the blissful hunger. For several moments Justice stood still and listened, waiting to see what would happen. But then Ember's mind seemed to give up the struggle and embraced the pleasure.

Justice immediately leapt forward and placed his hand on the dragon's scales.

"Ember, awake!"

Instantly, the dragon came alive with a screech at the jolt of fire and stumbled to his feet, trying to edge away.

Why! he seemed to nearly scream. *Why did you do that?*

"You were dreaming of Deception; you wanted him."

But why? the dragon seemed almost to beg, shaking his head. There was extreme mourning and pain in his voice. *You threatened to kill me if I ever see him again in life, why am I denied his comfort even in dreams?*

"Dreams arise from the desires of our hearts; what we allow ourselves to do in fantasy we will inevitably turn to in reality."

Ember shook his head again and turned away. *He's the only comfort I have left in this world; I hate that he uses it to enslave me, but I don't know how else to bear the pain. If you could generate a similar feeling in me instead of fire, then perhaps I would be able to draw from you instead.*

Justice shook his head angrily and began to gather his belongings. "No. I will not have you blindly following me because I give you some emotion. If you ever truly want to resist Deception, then you must become less dependent on feelings."

You're just saying that because you want me to return to him, then you won't need to rescue me. If you really wanted me to stay, why would you make it so hard?

"I do want to save you," said Justice, although he choked a little on the words as he said them. "If you come with me, I will help you, but you will have to follow my rules. I will not have a dragon by my side that's led only by something as frivolous and shifting as emotion. Learn to think for yourself."

Ember snorted. *All you bring is agony and pain. If you really desire to save me, then can you at least give me some incentive, any reason why I should go with you?*

Justice stared at him for a moment but then dropped his head. "I cannot," he said in a quieter voice. "I don't know how to help you. I honestly don't know how to do this at all; I didn't ask to be the Dragon Rider."

Ember looked at him, his eyes almost bearing a hint of compassion. *Then what do you suggest we do?*

"The only thing I can think of is to head east. The King told me that we might find help there."

Ember got to his feet. *Then we might as well get going. Mount me without your skin touching my scales if you can.*

Justice did so, and then the two of them turned to the rising sun.

They journeyed for a long while. The trees of the forest were thick and Ember traveled slowly without the benefit of flight. For hours they continued with neither saying much. Several times Justice glanced up at the sky and then back to the ground, wondering what Deception was doing and if he was tracking them. Throughout their travels he continued to feel pain and sadness within Ember; as the dragon constantly fought off thoughts of his former captive, thoughts that promised to bring him comfort and happiness, Justice almost began to feel pity for him.

Eventually the two came across a wide river running north to south. On the opposite side the ground quickly became dryer and the grass more scarce and tough. Ember eyed the scene oddly.

How is it that the makings of a desert can exist so close to water?

"Water is near, but the rains rarely fall here. See those mountains in the distance? They block rain clouds from the east; that and a constant wind can dry out the ground very quickly."

I see, said Ember. He still strained to see out into the vast plains. *What do you suppose we should be looking for?*

"I have no idea," admitted Justice. "Perhaps some lonely old hermit that can give us advice?"

Then we had better move on and start looking; the sun is beginning to set. Do you suppose there will be a crossing further upriver? It is too wide here to jump, and I cannot fly.

Justice eyed him oddly. "Why not just swim? You did it just yesterday when Deception escaped me."

Ember shook his head. *I hate water; I was mad with fear then and didn't realize what I was doing.*

"You hate water?" asked Justice incredulously. "Did you avoid it when you were with Peace?"

Yes, I did. He kept me out of rain and away from large bodies of water except when absolutely necessary. A distaste of water is a trait that all dragons share.

"I didn't know that," said Justice skeptically, turning Ember aside.

There are many things that you do not know about dragons, Ember said.

Justice remained silent.

The two of them traveled quite a way upriver before they found a place shallow enough to cross. Ember swam at several points, but for the most part he took pains to avoid the water that rose higher than his chest.

After crossing, Justice led Ember through the desert, seeking any-one or anything. But they found nothing—nothing except rocks, cracked ground, and a little sand. There were no houses, no towns, not even the smoke of a distant fire. Eventually night fell and Ember was forced to stop for the night. Justice found a spot between two small hills and a large rock pile that sheltered them from the wind that blew constantly from the east. They both settled down, Ember being quite exhausted from a long day of unaccustomed land travel. Even though it was very cold, Justice did not light a fire—he felt it too unsafe out in such an open, strange land.

I wonder how much longer we need to travel, thought Ember as he lay his head down between his forelegs and stared ahead.

"I can't tell," said Justice from where he sat on the ground. He looked up at the moon, a full crescent, and sighed. "I hope it's not much. The King warned me to reach him before the night of the full moon. We can't afford to stay another day." He lay down on his back and stared up at the many tiny stars, so high above.

Are you going to sleep? asked Ember. *You didn't last night.*

"I don't think so," said Justice. "The last time I allowed myself to take a decent rest my brother snuck away to his death. I've been afraid ever since then that if I slept too soundly, I would wake to lose something I hold dear." He turned to look at Ember and smiled slightly. "I guess that would be you now."

Ember snorted and closed his eyes. *You need not fear of losing me...that is unless Deception shows up here. If I dream of him again, will you wake me as you did before?*

"Yes, I will."

Ember shifted his head in discomfort and sighed a little. They were both silent for a while, and then Justice asked a question that had been on his mind since that morning.

"Why did you resist?"

Ember turned his head. *What?*

"In your dream last night, I felt you resist Deception. Why? I thought that you said you needed to feel his comfort again."

I do, said Ember sadly. *But yet, I knew that to follow him would be to leave you. I've already lost my former Rider, my King, my homeland...you're the only thing I have left of home.* He rolled his eyes and snorted. *Admittedly, you're the last thing from home I would have wanted, but regardless, you're all I have. I can't bring myself to lose you too.* He fell silent, and for a while neither spoke.

Then, quite suddenly, Justice sat up. "What's wrong?" he said.

What do you mean?

"I'm sensing you through the Link. Something is making you uneasy."

Ember raised his head and looked around, sniffing the air. *I didn't notice it before, but I think you are right. There appears to be something on the wind. It seems vaguely human, but also like something I cannot identify, almost as though someone were trying to cover up their scent.*

Justice quickly jumped to his feet and hurried up to the top of the hill to their east. He scanned the horizon but could see little in the dark. "That's odd," he said. "If someone wanted to mask their scent, why would they stand upwind? Wouldn't they know that any smell, regardless of how human it was, would attract a dragon's atten—"

With a sudden jolt, Justice whirled around. "Ember! Look out! It's a trap!"

Ember turned and immediately roared, blasting fire that lit up the dim night. There were men everywhere! Justice could see them darting left and right as the dragon tried to strike the small, swift targets. They moved with such speed and created such confusion together with their movements that Ember seemed unable to hit or even track any of them. Several outflanked him and hurled long chains over his back to waiting comrades on the other side.

Justice's hand flew to his sword hilt, but he never drew it because suddenly he found himself surrounded by five armed men. A sixth, who appeared to be their leader, sauntered up to him.

"Greetings, dragon owner," he stated nonchalantly. Behind him Justice could see men beginning to swarm his dragon.

Ember fought back viciously, struggling under the chains, sweeping with his tail, and trying to blast the elusive men with flame. *They're trying to run him out of fire!* Justice realized. But of course, Ember could not hear him.

"I know that you may find all of this a little difficult," said the man, "but we dragon trappers have to make our living somehow, especially when someone is paying a high price for the little beauties."

"Dragon trappers?" said Justice. "You work for Deception?"

The man smiled slyly. "It does not matter whom we serve. The point is that you have a dragon, and we are taking him off your hands. I suggest you just walk away...we might even reimburse you a little for your troubles."

Beyond the man, Justice continued to watch Ember struggle. It took three men at the end of each chain just to fight back against the dragon's strength. Several more men however were approaching with lassos of thick rope. They threw from both directions and several managed to snag Ember's neck, muzzle, and left horn. He growled fiercely and tried to pull the ropes out of their hands. The men fought back, five to a rope.

"You really should just leave," the man said, gesturing to Ember. "I know this might be hard for you, but you would need a license to have one of these anyway. Just leave and let us do our job."

Justice continued to stare straight ahead, almost as if stunned. His hand slowly went to his katana again.

"Ah, I wouldn't do that," said the man sternly.

Justice's eyes narrowed. "Let him go."

"Let him go." the man repeated in a mocking voice. "Are you going to make us? You and what army?"

There was a scuffle as Ember tried to keep his feet. He no longer could breathe fire because several well-aimed lassos had tightened around his jaws, effectively acting as a muzzle. The men were trying to pull him down onto his side, but Ember strained back with all his might. Beneath him, men darted between his legs with more chains, trying to break his stance.

Justice growled with rage and drew his sword. Around him the five men did the same.

The leader shook his head. "You think that you can overcome us? This is your last chance; leave or be killed!"

Justice crouched at the ready with his katana extended and drew his dagger with his other hand. His voice was cold, even, hard. "I'll tell you one last time: let him go!"

The man smiled and turned around. Behind him the trappers succeeded in breaking Ember's footing and he fell heavily on his side. Instantly he tried to get back up, but the men were swifter and swarmed him, throwing more chains over him, binding him to the ground. Several more men began to bind his foreclaws and hindlegs together with thick iron shackles. Ember moaned as his struggles grew weaker and more restricted. The leader turned back and smiled again at Justice, still surrounded by his five men.

"All right then; die well, dragon owner."

All five men moved in at once. But Justice's anger had been building to the breaking point and now it exploded with a speed and fierceness unlike anything ever before. Three swords were knocked aside by his first swing, and he ducked under the other two, rolling under their sweeps and slashing at unprotected legs. What happened next was a blur of flashing steel and arcing blades, but Justice was nearly livid with rage, and before he had blocked once and spun twice, he had risen with his sword bloodied and the five men dead around him. The leader looked at him shocked, visibly shaken.

Justice growled, his eyes blazing. "Die well, dragon trapper."

With a cry the man fled, but Justice charged after him, stopping his flight with a dagger. With hardly a glance Justice continued to run forward, only pausing to grab his weapon with one hand and to sweep out at a nearby solider with his sword before charging his fallen dragon. Around him men cried out and several tried to block his way, but Justice knocked them aside without a second glance. Leaping up and into the air he landed upon one of Ember's manacled foreclaws and then up and onto the dragon's side, thrusting men aside and knocking them off left and right.

He reached Ember's head a moment later, and after slaying one man and shoveling another to the ground, he slashed his sword across the ropes which bound Ember's muzzle.

"Free yourself!" he shouted as he battled three men down the dragon's neck.

Ember lifted his head, turned, and blasted the largest stream of fire he could at those holding him down with chains on one side. Justice leapt from his back and likewise battled those behind him, so that in a moment Ember was able to roll out from beneath his bonds. Men quickly tried to ensnare him again, but they seemed disorganized with Justice in their midst.

Purely by luck, Justice spotted a man with a key in the dim light and downed him with his dagger. Leaping over Ember's tail he soon had it in his possession and then turned around. Ember was desperately trying to get up as men swarmed all over him, but he couldn't seem to gain any footing on his bound feet.

Justice immediately ran for Ember's hindlegs—killing two men in his way—and wrestled with the key. It unlocked the manacles and Ember was able to roughly struggle upright. With a roar he swept the ground around Justice with his tail, knocking several men over, and then brought his head close to his foreclaws and breathed a long steady stream of fire over the shackles. The chain began to glow orange, then white, and then finally snapped. Now completely free, Ember begin to lash out at men left and right with claws, tail, and fire, leaping nimbly among his opponents to avoid being taken again.

Justice continued to battle fiercely with every man he came across. Their numbers, however, seemed only to be growing every minute and he quickly found himself fighting more and more at once. Then suddenly, when he was struggling with three men, an arrow flashed past his shoulder. Justice spun quickly around, trying to keep his attackers between himself and the archer, but it was of little use. The bowman continued to fire at him without thought to his comrades and Justice was soon forced to silence him with his dagger. Without a second weapon however, Justice was unable to grapple with more than one or two attackers at a time and he began to be forced backward.

The ground shook as he felt Ember leap to his side. Justice had half a second to react to his dragon's thoughts as Ember made a stance and began to swiftly blast fire around the two of them in a circle. But just as he was halfway through, his fire suddenly weakened, then died altogether in a plume of smoke, allowing their attackers to quickly regroup and charge through the break in the smoky barrier.

As Ember held back the brunt of the assault, Justice turned to run in the direction he had thrown his dagger. An arrow shot by him, and then three more, but he paid them no heed, his mind bent solely on retrieving his lost weapon. By the light of dying fires he caught the gleam of his dagger hilt still lodged in the man it had struck. With a leap he dove for it, grasped his blade, and sprang back up again in a fighting stance.

No swordsman came near, and Justice saw why. He had stumbled directly into a ring of archers, all poised and aiming their bows at him. He had just a moment to glance at all the glistening arrow tips before someone shouted a command and they all fired. At the same time, Ember leaped into the ring with a cry, rolling onto his side and curling around Justice to let his armored back take the blots. There was a shout and men quickly began to throw chains over the downed dragon.

"Get up!" Justice roared, turning to face the oncoming men. "They'll bind you down again if you don't get to your feet!"

Ember quickly struggled back up as several trappers attempted to clamber onto his scales. Lassos were thrown and one caught his horn, but Justice slashed through the rope immediately. Men began to swarm them and Ember moved to fight close at his master's side, but without his fire the trappers were becoming far bolder in their attacks. Justice could also feel that Ember was quickly tiring, his sleepless night and sudden exertion having sapped his energy reserves. As Justice battled fiercely with five then six men at a time, he could see that the dragon was beginning to leap a little more clumsily, to lash out a little more slowly. Exhaustion was overtaking him.

Justice knew that they had only one option left, and with as much speed as he could muster, he ducked and fought his way past his assailants to the dragon's side where he leaped to grab hold of one of the spikes on his back.

"Run!" he cried out. "Get out of here! Head toward the river!" Ember immediately turned, shook off several men trying to climb his neck, and charged in the direction he desperately hoped was toward the river.

Justice pulled himself up and began to fight his way up the dragon's back, knocking off any men along the way who had managed to hang on. Around him he began to hear the beating of horse hooves against the sand and turned to see a large number of trappers pursuing them. Quickly Justice made it to Ember's neck and redirected him slightly in his course. Men on horseback began to pull up on either side, twirling lassos. Several were hurled, two catching Ember's horn, but Justice quickly made his way up to slash them, shouting out: "Faster! Faster!"

With panting breath and thunderous footfalls that shook the ground, Ember pulled the last of his strength together and charged toward the river ahead, which glimmered in the moonlight.

I won't...have time...to swim it! he gasped.

Justice looked behind them at their pursuers and then turned back.

"Then you'll have to jump!" he shouted.

I won't make it...It's too far...

"You have to; it's the only way!" said Justice firmly. He held tightly onto one of Ember's spikes as the river approached, and then right as the dragon neared the bank, Justice placed his hand upon the back of Ember's neck giving him a flash of fire that jolted him into a powerful leap. They shot far out over the river, but it was clear that their speed would not be enough to make it. At the last moment, Ember quickly spread his wings to glide the remaining distance and screeched in pain as he tilted to the side, wind tearing through the injured wing.

Justice leaped from his back at the last moment and landed with a roll on solid ground, relatively unhurt. Ember however had entirely lost his balance and went careening into the earth on his side, plowing a short trench through the ground before coming to a stop.

Justice turned back to look at the opposite bank and found that the horsemen had skidded to a stop on the other side of the swiftly flowing river. They hollered and shouted in rage, waving their weapons, but then slowly turned around and rode back into the desert.

Justice fell on his back and breathed a great sigh of relief. "We did it!" he cried out with joy. "We made it Ember!"

Beside him, the dragon tried several times to pick himself up before

he managed to regain his feet. *We did? There're gone? Should we...head further away?* He limped over to Justice, one of his legs injured.

"No, I don't think they will follow," said Justice, walking over to the dragon's side. He was about to rest his hand on him, but then stopped knowing what his touch would bring. He turned away.

"They would need to head far upriver before finding a crossing, and by then we could be long gone. I don't think they will make the effort." He looked back and saw that the gash that marred Ember's left wing had been ripped about a foot longer. "Ember! Your wing!" he cried, running over to it. He ran his hand across the wound gently and Ember winced.

I think I will be all right. You saved me back there...it's the least I could do.

"You saved my life as well. Why did you so quickly lay down to guard me, knowing that it would likely cost you your freedom again?"

Ember shook his head. *I'm not sure. I didn't want to lose you and it just seemed to come over me all at once.*

Justice nodded. He didn't say so, but he had felt something similar.

Ember stumbled slightly and turned, looking around. *I need to rest; I won't be able to stand much longer otherwise. Are you sure that we should not move somewhere else?*

Justice nodded and the two of them moved a bit away from the river to the shelter of some trees. Ember immediately laid down and struggled to find a position that was comfortable for his injured leg and wing. Justice sat beside him.

Do you think that we will need to go back? Ember asked. *We never found the help that your father described.*

Justice leaned back against the dragon's side and stared out at the river. "Actually, I think we did," he said. He shook his head and smiled inwardly to himself. *He knew there would be dragon trappers there,* he thought quietly. *He knew that both of us, being military minded, would be forced to work together in the event of an attack.* He shook his head. *What a sly fox he was.*

Aye, a very sly fox indeed.

Justice spun around.

You heard me?

Yes I did; it appears that you have chosen to be bonded to me.

And you?

I did during the attack; I decided that if you really were the last link I had to home, then I would follow and protect you to the end.

Justice turned and stared up at the stars. He realized that somewhere in the chaos, he too had unknowingly made a similar choice—a choice to guide Ember and fight for him even until death. He smiled. *Does this mean that we need to say the Pledges of Loyalty to each other?*

I don't see how that is possible, especially since the King is not here for you to make yours. But regardless, I want you to know that I am sorry. I'm sorry for resisting you, for desiring Deception, for...for what I did to Peace and to Highland. I want you to know that I will do anything I can to make up for it and right the wrongs I caused, that I would be more than willing to follow you. I place myself at your service. For what it's worth, I am your dragon.

Justice smiled again. *And for what it's worth, I am your Rider. I know that I'm not Peace, and that I can never become what he was, but as far as I am able to, I will try to help you escape this place and ensure that you see your homeland one more time.*

Ember nodded sadly and laid his head down between his claws. *Yes...one more time.*

Soon he was asleep, and at his side Justice slept soundly.

3

Travels

In the darkness of night, under the shadow of a forest tree, a figure lingered, waiting with a saber at its side. Another man approached and stood at attention.

The figure turned to him and spoke. "What have you to report?"

"The tame dragons are getting rare; nearly all that were domestically hatched in the manner you prescribed have been found and returned to you. Only one did we find in the past three weeks—and it escaped."

"Escaped?"

"Yes. We very nearly had it, but its owner guarded it. I lost my best officer to him."

"But surely your men could have overwhelmed them."

"They fought fiercely together; and commander—"

"What is it?"

"The dragon had a torn left wing."

The figure's eyes widened. "Tell me! What color was it?"

"Green, like that of an emerald."

"And you lost them! Do you have any idea who they were?!"

"Yes sire; I believe that they were the ones whom you have been seeking. I thought however that they were no longer necessary for your plans."

"They are not, but that does not mean that I would have them running free throughout my country! Do you know where they are now?"

"No sire, but—"

"But what?"

"—I do know where they will be soon."

The figure's head turned in surprise. The man held out a piece of paper.

"They left in such a hurry that the owner forgot his saddlebag. In it we found two letters—one addressed from the King!"

The figure snatched the paper from his hand and quickly scanned it by the dim light of the moon. Then he looked up. "They are traveling north to meet the King at the battlefield...and before the night of the full moon. Interesting..."

"That will take them through Sorrow's Pity. You can capture them there."

"But why wait? They can be intersected along the way."

"Then shall I ready my men?"

"No!" the figure barked. "You and your men have failed me for the last time." He smiled cruelly. "This time, I will handle them myself!"

***

Ember struggled in his sleep. Guilt and pleasure, sorrow and comfort clashed within his subconscious. Part of him began to realize what was happening, and his confused, muddled mind tried to pull away. He fought back and forth, trying to summon the will to resist, and then suddenly his dream snapped and he jerked awake with a start.

Instantly the feeling, previously indistinct and hidden within the confines of his dream, flared awake with full power. Ember nearly doubled over as he was hit with a wave of not pain but indescribable sadness, as though he were listening to a heartbreaking melody. The sadness, the sorrow seemed to drown him as he desperately longed for the only cure he knew: Deception's touch. But then he jerked away, feeling in his mind the consciousness of another man, one whose very presence seemed to radiate fire.

Desperately Ember tried to call himself back, to remember who he was, to fight off the pain that drove him to desire comfort. But the pain did not easily regress. He fought it, but somehow it grew sadder as it grew weaker—as if it were some injured animal that did not complain as it was stabbed, but rather looked up heartbroken to ask why. And as it died, Ember felt it jerk at his heart, as though he were the one dying. The feeling was not impossible to fight, but it was not something he desired to fight; it made him want to give up, to let himself fall into self-pity. And beneath it all there was the longing—the longing for that something that just couldn't be named, but yet pleadingly, beseechingly begged to be filled. Something that Deception alone could give.

Ember jerked back against it and called out: *Justice! Justice, I need you!* Immediately he felt a stab of fire that seemed to course through him all at once, blasting through the sorrow and killing it with a piercing scream. Ember leaped back instinctively and tried to get ahold of himself as the pain slowly faded. He saw Justice before him, obviously waiting since the start of the dream. Had Ember been in a calmer state of mind he might have seen that as a sign of caring, but now it seemed only like cruelty.

"That's the third time this night, and you have yet to fight it off without me."

I wish I could! Ember snapped. He shook his head and started to settle down a little. *Why does your touch sting? Peace's never did.*

Justice turned and walked back to the fire he had been stoking. Dawn was beginning to break in the east. "Because that's how a wound reacts to being sterilized. Darkness shutters and dies before the light."

Ember turned, shaking his head, and extended his giant wings halfway. The torn edges of the gash had healed but had not joined back together, leaving his left wing still marred by the great tear. Justice looked at it and a flicker of emotion flashed across his face. He looked back down. "I'm afraid that will never heal. It looks like you may be grounded for life, my friend."

Ember folded his wings and stared down toward the ground. A tear formed in his eye. *Why am I so broken?* he asked. *Why can I not control my own feelings? Why do my own dreams fight against me? They remembered Peace when I was still in captivity.*

"That was because then your memories and natural instincts were not yet accustomed to Deception's influence. Now they remember him."

How long will it take before they disappear?

Justice chuckled slightly. "Oh, they will never disappear; we are always stained by the effects of what we live through. Its intensity may decrease with time, but that depends on how hard you fight it."

And how long will that take?

Justice looked up at him. "I may be able to speed the process. My touch feels like fire only because Deception's influence still rests in you and it recoils from me. If you allowed me to hold my hand on you, I might succeed in burning a good deal of it away."

Ember eyed him distastefully and snorted. *And how long would I need to endure your pain?*

"I cannot say. Afterward though, my hand may sting less."

I'm not ready for that now, grunted Ember, his body still throbbing from the fire only a few minutes before. *Let's continue heading north.*

"As you wish," said Justice, mounting carefully to avoid touching his scales, and the two of them turned and began to travel.

And so they rode for several days, but the going north was long and tedious. The leg Ember had hurt in the attack had healed, but the long hours of travel by land wearied him and forced them to stop each night. Every time Ember slept, he awoke with the sorrow and the longing burning inside of him, sometimes two or three times a night. Justice's touch stung worse each time he brought him back, and Ember began to grow tired and irritable. Still they continued to press on.

Eventually the two of them came to a dense wood where the trees grew so close together that Justice was unable to lead his dragon through. With time running out they had to make a detour west toward the sea in order to go around. They eventually came to a marsh, which would've taken Ember only a day to cross by air, and were forced to spend three nights in it as the dragon struggled to pull himself through the thick mud. Without his ability to fly, Ember was also incapable of catching his own prey and Justice was forced to go out alone time and time again to catch meals for them both.

I feel so helpless! Ember growled on the night of the second day. *Before, I was a blessing to my Rider. I would fly Peace for miles and we would cover distance faster than anyone. Here however I only slow you down.*

"Don't be too hard on yourself," said Justice sympathetically. "You belong naturally to Tarenthia. It is your country and you flourish there. Here you are out of place and burdened with the weight of other matters. You will thrive again when we return."

If I live, you mean, said Ember sourly.

"What are you talking about?"

You are going to kill me remember? What good does it do me to thrive when I return?

Justice looked at him sharply and his eyes narrowed. "Look, I no longer relish the idea of your execution, but the law is the law. I have sworn my life to enforcing it; I cannot go back on the justice of Highland—that would be treason itself."

Ember turned his head away and said nothing, but his tail swished angrily over the muddy grass.

And so the two of them traveled on. The moon was half full when they finally made it out of the swamp, and Justice began to urge them on more and more each day as their time fell to one week, and then less than a week. The going did become faster however, and Ember was able to spare more time to rest, although his sleep was continually broken by dreams.

One night, Justice left Ember alone for a few hours to travel to a nearby village and learn the lay of the land. When he returned, he found his dragon lost in thought. Justice eyed him oddly, noting how quiet Ember had become in the past few days.

"What is the matter?" he asked.

Ember turned his head to him. *When I was with Deception, he told me many things. But he did not always lie, and I can't distinguish between what is true and what is false.*

"Then ask me," offered Justice, sitting down to start a fire. "I won't lie to you."

Ember nodded and settled down as though trying to think of a question.

He told me that Peace hated me, that he did not want me after I left.

"That is false," said Justice, probing the fire with a stick. "He died trying to save you—you know that."

He also told me that hunger is better than love, because it always promises more.

"False. Hunger may provide more pleasure, but that does not make it better."

He told me that I was genetically altered by Highland before my birth.

The stick stopped probing. Justice stared silently at the fire as if deciding how to answer that question.

"True," he said at length.

He told me that Highland submerges dragon eggs in cold water to make the hatchlings within more submissive and dependent. He said that Highland used the technique to control its dragons.

"True, on both accounts."

Then I am not a natural dragon; I was implanted with the desire to be controlled.

"That is correct."

Ember eyed him quizzically. *If all of this it true, then why are you telling me these things?*

"It would be a mighty odd thing indeed if it were found that Justice had lied to you while Deception told the truth, would it not?"

Ember laid his head back down. *I guess so. Tell me: did Peace know?*

"Yes, he did. It is tradition, however, that the Rider not tell his dragon of its origin until the bond between them grows too great to break. He might have told you in a few more years."

Then I have been a slave all my life; even Peace was my captor.

"Yes, I suppose you could say that."

Ember was silent for a moment.

Can I ever go back?

"No, the change is permanent; it cannot be reversed."

Ember looked at him sadly, betrayed, and then turned away. *Tell me,* he said at length. *What is my kind like? What is it like to be one of the unbroken dragons?*

"Well, I have never been one, but I can tell you what we have observed."

Please do.

Justice nodded. "The free dragons live wild in the north of our old land, although they seem to live in greater abundance here. They are proud, and unconquerable. They have no weaknesses, no obligations, and no debts; they live independent of all cares and masters. A wild dragon is impossible to tame; even Deception would be unable to break through to them. They are fearless, courageous, and...sad."

Ember looked oddly up at him, but Justice was staring out into space as if remembering something from long ago.

"They live their daily lives in pain, in a sort of madness. It appears that a wild dragon is so predisposed to fight, to protect itself, that it is incapable of giving its heart to anything else, making it therefore incapable of love. They are their own masters, cursed for their lifetime, and trapped within a reality where there is no purpose or meaning aside from preserving their own miserable existence."

So, they are enslaved even still?

"Yes, with their own freedom. They are built with power, with fire, and with every ability to cherish and protect but without an object to cherish or protect. They cannot give themselves up. Our method in Highland however has quite the opposite effect. Our dragons cannot *help* giving themselves up, although they may choose whom to devote themselves to. In either case, both kinds of dragons are led by the same passions and desires...but one has the gift of choice, even if it then *must* choose. It has to be one way or the other; there is no way to change a dragon after it has hatched, so the choice is ours and must be made without the knowledge or consent of the dragon itself."

I see, said Ember, and then he was quiet for a moment as he thought.

"The only reason we have dragon eggs at all," continued Justice, "is because one of our kings tried to speak to your race long ago. Many refused him, several tried to kill him, but one sad and lonely female who was tired of her pointless and directionless life listened. The king at that time convinced her to come down with him to his kingdom where she laid the first dragon eggs. She gave them to us in hopes that her offspring might know a better life than she had. Then she flew off, her nature driving her on, and was killed several years later by another dragon."

So, you would have me believe that breaking me at my birth was an act of mercy?

"That is up to you to decide what to believe. Every dragon, however, once told by its Rider, has held no resentment toward their origin. But your opinion is yours to make."

Ember was silent for a while longer, staring out at the ground ahead of him and then up at the glittering stars. Justice did not say anything more but turned his gaze upward as well to look upon the jeweled heavens and the waxing half-moon.

I do not regret what has been done to me, Ember said at last. *I was at peace with my old Rider, and that peace was worth the enslavement. Now, however, since he is gone, the burden of whom to follow is crushing. If I follow you I choose death, and if I follow Deception I gain you as an enemy...and either way I bear the responsibility. I wish I did not have to choose.*

But without choice, what are you? Justice said to him through the Link. *You are like the rocks and the other animals that only react to their environment. They have no life, they have no soul...only choice can give you that.*

Ember nodded and continued to stare up at the sky. *May I ask you one more question?*

Of course.

This feeling I have, that Deception seems to create and satisfy all at the same time; what is it? What do I desire so greatly but can never seem to grasp?

Justice was quiet for a time, and when he spoke, he spoke out loud.

"You want to know what the feeling is? You desire comfort. You desire to be crushed with sorrow and pain, all while knowing that another pities you. You long to lie injured on a cold night and know that another is protecting you. You desire to have your heart broken so that you can trust it to another to soothe. In short, you long to give someone your very soul, to give it for them to take and handle gently even though it gives them the power to destroy you." Justice looked up at Ember, who turned to face him, and smiled softly.

"You also long for the opposite—to be the one that pities and helps the broken, that guards the injured, that soothes the brokenhearted. You long to be the one entrusted with the very heart and essence of another, and to guard it tenderly and shield it from all harm. In short, what you desire is to be loved and to love in return."

Ember cocked his head at him. *Is that what love is?*

"No," chuckled Justice, turning back to his fire. "Though it is similar. Love is sacrificing yourself for another, and typically you will entrust your soul to one whom you feel will do that for you. The desire to give the essence of who you are into the hands of another provides motivation for love and the comfort received from it the incentive, but love itself is an action separate from either. Your desire to shield and comfort, and to be shielded and comforted, is natural to all tamed dragons and to all humans as well. It's just the way we are; it's as if in pursuing the fulfillment of the longing, we would be taught what love is, and then to love beyond our feelings."

But why must I have this desire? growled Ember. *Why must I long to be ruled by another? It's a weakness that makes me so easy to control.*

"It is still up to you to decide whom you give control to," said Justice sternly, "but the desire is present in all of us. We were meant to give our souls to another; if we try to carry them too long ourselves, they grow heavy. That is why I gave mine to the call of justice instead of to something that can be killed or broken, but even a cause will begin to control you if you give yourself to it—or so I have found..."

But if this hunger is natural in me, said Ember. *Then why could I never figure it out? Why did it always elude me?*

"Because you wanted it to."

I did?

"Yes, and that is Deception's work. The desire you had to be ruled was always inside of you; Deception did not create it, he only brought it to the surface. What he *did* do however was make you enjoy hungering for it."

How can one be made to want hunger?

"You know yourself that hunger is, in a twisted way, a type of pleasure. Anticipation borrows joy from the future; it excites, empowers! But it is also destructive. You never figured out what it was because you knew, in the back of your mind, that your longing would disappear if it finally found its target."

But it is such a sick and destructive pleasure. How could I have been fooled into living by it?

"Deception himself lives by it, and that is because he believes that the meaning of life is to seek pleasure. So he has spent his life looking for ways to create it, to extend it. He decided that hunger was the most consistent, reliable source that he could manufacture. Happiness is a natural part of life, but it was never meant to be our primary aim; when taken outside its purpose, pleasure will—like all other things—naturally become twisted, which is why Deception now thinks that perfect bliss can only be found in something as destructive as perpetual desire."

Is there a way that I can escape this longing, this hunger to give my soul to him?

"You could let me purge it from you," offered Justice, holding up his hand. "It would lessen the effect."

The dragon's eyes narrowed and he snorted in disgust. *No; your fire would kill me.*

"Then you will need to learn to control it yourself," said Justice.

Ember grunted and turned away. Soon they were both asleep.

* * *

The next day they resumed travel early in the morning. Ember seemed to be in a better mood than the previous night, but for the most part he was quiet, thinking about what had been said. Justice was also silent, guiding his dragon as they continued along. The night of the full moon was only five days away, and Justice still didn't know exactly how much farther they would need to travel. Ember asked him if he had learned much about the road ahead from the village he had visited, but Justice gave only a short reply. Ember sensed something in the back of his Rider's mind that he seemed to be both hiding and burdened by. He decided, however, against asking what it was.

As the sun was setting, the two of them broke through the trees and into a very large clearing. On the north side the flat ground disappeared suddenly in a sheer drop, leaving nothing but open air beyond. When Ember lumbered over to it, they found that they had reached the edge of a cliff, maybe fifty to seventy feet high, that looked out over an enormous cove formed from the sea to the west.

Did you know about this place? asked Ember.

No, I did not, said Justice. *It appears that the sea cuts inland here, blocking our way.*

Out ahead, beyond the cove, another forest could be seen springing up on the banks of the northern shore. Had Ember been able to fly, they could have glided the distance in a few minutes. Now it proved a nearly impossible barrier.

Should we go around? asked Ember at length.

Unless you want to swim that, I see no alternative. A trip around, however, could take up to three days and we'll need that time for later... And Ember once again felt the disturbance of Justice's hidden burden. But then in a moment it was gone, and he said: *Why don't we stay here for the night? It's too late to do much more anyway, and then we can decide tomorrow after there has been more time to think about it.*

Ember agreed and the two retreated back into the woods to make camp amidst the shelter of the trees.

The evening passed slowly and uneventfully. Justice left to hunt, and Ember dozed off briefly. He was awakened by the longings, but he fought hard against them and was able to recover by the time his Rider returned. Justice seemed pleased, but he didn't say much and the two of them soon went to sleep.

In the middle of the night, Ember was awakened by Justice shaking his head gently by the horn. Ember grunted and turned to his Rider. *What is it?*

Lay still and be quiet; Deception is here.

He is? Where?

Justice pointed out toward the clearing. Between the trees, Ember could see that the open space was now filled with tents and with men walking around campfires. In the center lay the largest tent, and before it stood Deception, giving orders. Two large dragons lay at the far side of the clearing next to the cliff edge. They seemed at ease but were awake and attentive. Ember turned back to Justice.

Have they seen us?

Apparently not. We must be far enough in the woods that the darkness hides us.

I'm surprised.

So am I. Shouldn't the other dragons be able to smell you?

I would have thought. Maybe because there are already two of them, they think that they are only sensing each other. What do we do now?

Nothing. We will have to wait and see if they leave in the morning.

But couldn't we take the chance to attack them? What if we wait until most of them are asleep, and then charge them together? We could kill Deception before he even knows we're here, and then escape before the men awake. We could both be rid of the man that killed your brother and my former Rider!

No, we must not, said Justice. *I want that man dead as much as you do, but I will not risk losing you again. And where would we escape to? The dragons would stop us before we even had the chance to get away.*

No, they wouldn't. If they are anything like I was, they'll be so distraught by Deception's death that we should easily be able to get away. And besides, together we can overcome anything! What use is a Dragon Rider pair if they do not use their power for good when they have the chance?

No, Ember; a Dragon Rider pair derives its power from patience and wisdom in addition to its strength. And we are far from being able to overcome anything.

Ember eyed him angrily. *You think I'll be taken again, don't you? You think I'll be overcome, even after the progress I've made in fighting him off.*

You have made progress, my friend, but you still do not know the desires of your own soul like I do. Much of Deception's influence still rests in you.

Ember snorted softly. *You still don't trust me! How can you doubt my loyalty?*

It is not your loyalty I doubt, said Justice, reaching out to touch Ember's snout. The dragon shied away from the heat of his hand. *But there is still much darkness in your heart. Please trust me; I vowed to try and get you safely to the King—trust me to do that.*

Ember grunted but lay still. At length, Justice sat down beside him and as the night progressed he slowly fell asleep. But the dragon did not. He stayed up long after his Rider had drifted off, thinking about the man who now rested no more than thirty yards away, oblivious to their presence. He thought back to the time of his imprisonment, to what Deception had done to him. And he had other dragons as well; how many more of Ember's own kind had been treated like himself? Ember growled and anger boiled inside of him. The man deserved to die! Why didn't Justice see that? This was their chance; Deception would run at any other time, but now he could not. He was asleep; the other dragons were asleep; the men were asleep. It was perfect.

Slowly, Ember rose from the ground being careful not to disturb Justice. The camp lay quiet and peaceful before him. Energy and anticipation seemed to pulse through his body. It would be so easy to do; he could charge right in, set fire to the camp, and kill the man before anyone even had a chance to awake. He could do it! Ember was at the edge of the clearing now. His body shivered in excitement. He would do it! The so-called Dragon Tamer would be killed by one of his own dragons. How fitting!

Ember crouched, ready to spring forward. Adrenalin rushed through him, but the strength of his emotions bothered him. Quickly, Ember tried to distinguish where they came from. He felt longing and hunger to...to...his mind raced and made it difficult to think. In a moment he would be before Deception for the last time. Yes, of course, for the last time. He would be dead after this. A pity, really.

Ember shook his head. Something was wrong, but he couldn't think of it—didn't want to think of it. He just wanted to charge. He could do it! What was he waiting for? He was the Rider's dragon after all! Ember moaned softly, trying to force his way through the torrent blasting through his head. And then something, perhaps a last-ditch effort sprung by the back of his mind, caused him to look back at Justice one more time. He stared at his Rider, a pang of guilt stabbing through his heart, and the torrent of feelings seemed to subside a little.

It was then that Ember decided that he would not do it. His body cried out in protest, but his heart suddenly felt at peace. Quietly, Ember made his way back to his master's side and lay down. He still desperately wanted to rush out against Deception, but too much of his longing seemed to be hunger. Ember closed his eyes and began to calm down.

All right Justice, I will trust you. I hope that someday, however, you will allow me to rise up with you against him. And then Ember slept.

* * *

Both Rider and dragon awoke just on the verge of dawn. The morning was dark and still; there was no sound.

There're gone, said Justice as he looked out through the trees.

Really? To where? asked Ember with surprise. He rose and peered out into the clearing. It seemed mostly deserted. The tents were still there, and a few campfires still smoldered weakly, but there was not a soul to be seen.

What happened? asked Ember.

Justice was just as confused. *It appears that they left with great haste. I wonder if something scared them.*

Or maybe they thought they saw us, and ran off into the woods.

It's very curious indeed. Let me look around first, to make sure no one is here.

Slowly, Justice crept out into the open, his katana in hand. In the dim light, Ember watched from the trees as he advanced into the center and looked around. He turned back, his face confused.

It seems that this place really has been abandoned, he said. *You can come out.*

Ember slowly broke cover and advanced forward.

Justice continued to look around. *I wonder if they—*

Suddenly there was a screech and Ember whirled around barely in time to see the dark shapes of two dragons diving from the skies. There were cries and Ember turned again to see men charging at Justice from the abandoned tents, weapons raised. Then Ember was hit with the force of a battling ram as the dragons collided into him.

For just a second, Ember felt despair. They had been tricked; they would both be captured. But his despair lasted only a moment. With a flash of determination, Ember's spirit returned and he kicked at the dragons with a deep growl, knocking one of them off. The second snapped at his neck but Ember struck back, blasting fire. As he grappled with his opponent in the dim light, Ember sensed the other one approaching and lashed out with his tail blindly, feeling it hit something that cracked.

Then both were upon him and all was a chaos of wings and claws and deep-throated growls as Ember struggled desperately against their overwhelming power. He received several minor wounds to his underbelly and a slash across his injured wing before managing a solid strike against one of his opponents' heads. For just a moment he felt himself freed and he desperately spun around, choking on the smoke. Where was Justice?

Suddenly he was hit again and Ember was knocked onto his back, feeling teeth against the scales of his shoulder. He tried to shake his opponent off, but then the other dragon was upon him as well, pinning him to the ground. Ember struggled vainly under their crushing weight, but could not move. Through the swirling smoke, he made out the snarling faces of the two dragons as they bore down on him, their claws against his chest. They were both obviously bigger than he and had far more experience battling their own kind. But he was the Rider's dragon, and his will to fight ran deeper!

Determination boiling within him, Ember blinded his assailants with a barrage of flame and kicked out violently with his hind legs. They made contact with one of the dragon's stomachs and the beast was knocked aside, howling in agony.

Instantly, Ember was at the throat of the other as he rolled over, broke free, and slashed out wildly, scoring several hits against its scales. They fought viciously, rising up on their hind legs and roaring like lions, but the other dragon was stronger and began to push him back. Thinking quickly, Ember ducked and shifted his weight to the side, causing his assailant to stumble and lose its footing. Jumping lightly around and into the open, Ember attempted to leap up upon his opponent's back to hold him down, but was knocked nearly senseless as the other dragon landed a heavy blow against his head with its spiked tail.

Ember stumbled as the world spun, and a moment later one of the dragons rammed itself into his side, claws scratching his injured wing. With a roar that sounded more like a moan, Ember swung blindly with his own tail and managed a lucky hit on the second dragon's head, causing it to fall to the ground stunned.

Ember could feel his strength waning now. The other dragon was overpowering him, and the ground still rocked too dizzily for him to even attempt to get to his feet. His fire was running low and he choked on the smoke that seemed to be everywhere. Desperately, thoughts of his Rider urging him on, Ember pulled together the last of his might and pushed back against the dragon on top of him. It rolled to the side and then—perhaps because it saw that its companion had still not regained its feet—leaped into the air unfurling its enormous wings.

Immediately Ember was up, adrenalin running through him as he saw his chance. He roared much louder than before, blasted fire that lit up the night sky, and leapt with all his power. He locked his jaws around the dragon's neck and pulled its body down under his weight, feeling the beast crash into the earth with tremendous force. It groaned, trying to get back up, but Ember struck it in the head and knocked the dragon senseless. With both of his assailants momentarily unresponsive, Ember quickly turned, the last of his fire blazing in his throat, to the center of the clearing, calling out to his Rider.

He stopped with shock. Justice was being held captive by four soldiers, while several men with crossbows stood stationed around him, their bows at the ready. Around them lay the bodies of those Justice had slain, but now his weapons were in the hands of the men and one had even taken his Link.

Between Ember and the knot of soldiers stood Deception.

4

Sorrow's Pity

Ember growled, baring his teeth, and tried to summon his fire. But it caught in his throat, just as he feared it would if used against the man. Deception drew forth a little red horn and sounded it. Instantly fear raced through Ember and he nearly turned to run, but then he locked his eyes on Justice and forced his way through the torrent until it subsided.

Deception looked up at him and smiled.

"Ah, so you have overcome your fear! You are the first—you have become worthy of my highest respect."

Behind him, Ember heard the other dragons regaining their feet and starting to approach, but Deception stopped them with a wave of his hand.

"Really, Ember, you have grown strong; I was surprised that you did not take the chance to join me last night. I thought striking camp close by would give you the opportunity you needed to escape this captor of yours." He gestured to Justice in a dismissive sort of way.

Ember growled. *He is not my captor; you are! You are the one who held me prisoner against my will with a Curse!*

"Yes, and what a sad mistake that was," said Deception with regret, slowly advancing forward. "I see now that I should never have done that; but it showed me how strong you are when you broke through!"

Get away from me! Ember roared, blowing a little smoke to make his point clear. Deception stopped. *You lie! You always have! It was Peace who saved me from your Curse, not myself!*

Deception looked up to Ember curiously, and then took a step back. "Okay; you think I lie? Then test my statements with sound logic; hear my reason and know for yourself that I speak the truth. Tell me, which of us has threatened you with death if you were to leave? Is it not Justice? I can feel it in your mind; you still fear what he plans to do with you. But as for me—even before the Curse, you stayed with me of your own will. I would have let you go had you asked. How am I the one who imprisons?"

Ember looked back and forth between Deception and Justice, trying to fight off the influence of his words. He looked to Justice for help, but his master said nothing, watching the exchange in silence.

"You see!" cried Deception. "Even he does not deny it! Search him, my Ember; tell me if he feels anything for you, if he desires you at all! He hates you; the very justice inside of him screams out against you. He wants you dead—and it's taking him everything just to wait until you are before the King. Ask him if what I say is true!"

Ember turned to his Rider again and he nodded slightly.

"What Deception says about me is correct," said Justice without expression.

"You see!" cried Deception again. "He has no desire for you; he does not love you!"

It's a trick, growled Ember boldly. *You know nothing about him!*

"But Ember," said Deception, taking a step forward again. "I can feel the pain he has caused you, the joy he has kept from you. And I am deeply saddened by it. Can't you feel my pain for you? For all of the dragons Highland has enslaved? I want to free them. That is why I came to you: to end Highland's rule of oppression. Yes, I had planned to kill you before, as you were part of the old age, but now I see my mistake. Come with me and I will make you the shining symbol of the new order! We will free your kind!"

What Highland did has already freed us! said Ember, backing away. *Would you have all dragons living their lives in misery, unable to love or devote themselves to anything?*

"Of course not!" said Deception with concern. "I do not wish to end Highland's method, but to perfect it! I want only to wait until we find a way to let the *dragon* choose its state of mind, instead of having it chosen by others before its birth. Is that not the *right* thing to do? Are my motives not just?"

Deception was very close now. Ember shied away. *Get away!* he said weakly. *You lie! You do not care for me; you only want to help yourself.*

"But I *do* care for you!" cried Deception. "Don't you know how much I desire you? How much I long for all dragons? I am devoted to your kind; I wish so badly to be reunited with you. Don't you remember how fond I was of you? How I visited and spoke with you alone in the quiet nights? How you were my very own dragon chosen from so many? Please, come to me again. I want to put a stop to the pain that causes you to tremble. I long to give you the love you so greatly desire; won't you give me the chance?"

They were face-to-face now. Deception had his hand raised and it was only inches from Ember's muzzle. Desperately Ember looked to Justice but he remained silent, still watching.

"Do not worry about him," said Deception soothingly. "He cannot hurt you now."

Why don't you say anything? Ember asked his Rider pleadingly, although of course he wouldn't hear without his Link. *Why do you say nothing in your defense?* Then suddenly, as if prompted by his memory, words came to his mind.

It would be a mighty odd thing indeed if it were found that Justice had lied to you while Deception told the truth...

The words seemed to drift through Ember's head as he stared at Deception's hand. Then he stopped and cocked his head.

No, he said, a thought suddenly striking him. *Wait just a minute...*

"What is it?" asked Deception with concern.

Justice gives no defense. He's letting me choose.

"See?" said Deception. "He does not care for you! He's willing to lose you!"

No, said Ember, beginning to smile inwardly. *He's willing to let me go.* He turned back to Deception, excitement rising in his eyes. *He refuses to lie, even when the truth works against him. He continues to make his touch burn like fire, even though it is hard for me to bear. At every turn he does what is best for me, even knowing that I might hate him for it.*

"Ember, please. You are confused. Think about this logically; use your reason."

You want me to use reason? Ember growled. *Fine, here are the facts: Justice has stayed behind in order to seek me, he fights his own sense of justice to leave me alive, and he is even willing to do things that may affect my loyalty if they are in my best interest. He is willing to love me even when it may cause me to hate him in return.*

"Ember, please..."

But you, he growled, beginning to advance a little himself, and causing Deception to retreat before him. *When have you been willing to sacrifice my loyalty? When have you acted out of my best interest even when it might incline me to turn against you? When have you loved me even though you may get nothing in return? Everything you have ever done has been to make me like you, hunger for you, desire you. Why should I believe you care for me?*

"But I do care for you!" cried Deception pleadingly. "Everything I have done has been for your best interest!"

And oddly enough, my best interest has always seemed to be those things that made me more dependent on you.

"You *wanted* to be dependent on me! If you think I do not care for you, then ask anything from me and you'll see that I'll do it!"

All right, said Ember slowly. He leaned his head in close. *Then this I request of you: let Justice go free.*

"But—but...Ember..."

If you really do care for me, then let us both go. Highland may have enslaved their dragons, but at least they always gave us the freedom of choice. Will you do that? Will you let me choose?

Deception backed away slowly, shaking his head. "No, my Ember, you do not understand what you are asking."

Ember crouched and growled. *I said to let us go!*

Deception placed his hand on his saber. "No, my friend; I'm afraid I cannot allow that." Behind him, Ember sensed the two other dragons crouching on either side, preparing to pounce. Deception drew his weapon and grinned sadly. "I guess I just love you too much to let him take you." He raised his sword high above his head. Ember tensed. "Do not worry," he said. "You will understand soon. I will see to that."

He brought the saber down.

Instantly both dragons sprang for Ember. But Ember leaped forward at the same time, sailing over Deception's head to land in the group of men that held Justice captive. Archers fired, but Ember blasted flame all around and they retreated. Then the other two dragons were upon him, grappling with him on either side and trying to pull him down. Desperately, Ember craned his neck around to one of the beasts and sank his teeth into its wing. With a cry the dragon fell from him, roaring out in agony and pain. Ember quickly threw his weight against the other dragon and temporarily freed himself.

Justice by this time had retrieved his weapons and Link in the confusion and now leapt onto his back. "Run!" he cried, and Ember quickly released the dragon's wing and burst forward.

"You fool!" cried Deception. "You will be destroyed! Just wait; he'll betray you the first chance he gets!"

Ember did not listen; instead he charged forward as the two dragons began to pursue.

"The cliff! Head to the cliff!" cried Justice, and Ember adjusted his course accordingly.

One of the other dragons roared, and just as they were about to reach the edge it leaped at them, latching onto Ember's side. The other joined and Ember struggled desperately under their weight. Then Justice, moving quickly, reached out and touched the scales of the closest dragon. Instantly the beast reacted with a screech and fell back. Ember, with a final burst of strength shook off the other dragon and lurched forward, diving over the edge of the cliff.

They plummeted straight downward like a missile, the rocky wall of the precipice shooting past them in a blur. In the new light of the rising sun, the water below first glittered as they approached and then exploded as they entered. The momentum of their fall carried Ember a good distance downward before he was able to turn and struggle back to the surface, kicking violently against the water. They broke up into the open air and both Justice and Ember gasped for breath.

"The shore! Make for the shore!" cried Justice. Ember sputtered and tried to point himself north.

I can't make it! It's too far!

"No, you can!" said Justice gently but firmly. "Just concentrate on the water directly ahead of you. Don't stop swimming!"

Ember gulped and began to paddle. In the sky above, one of the dragons, the one whose wing Ember had not injured, rocketed over the cliff edge and began to search for them.

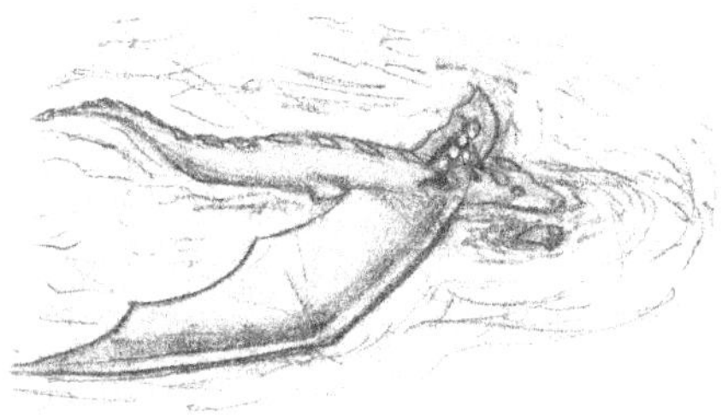

It's one of them! He'll kill us both! cried Ember desperately.

"No!" barked Justice. "I will take care of him. Just concentrate on swimming."

Ember looked forward and continued to tread water. The dragon above spotted them and began to dive, screeching.

"Get ready to duck underwater," said Justice as the creature came for them, fire forming in its throat. He braced himself, tense and at the ready. The other dragon blasted its flame.

"Now!" cried Justice and immediately Ember dove. He kicked downward several lengths and Justice, hanging onto one of his dragon's spikes, looked up to see the red and orange flame blossom against the surface of the water. Then Ember struggled back up into the air and Justice saw the dragon off in the distance beginning to circle.

"Keep going!" he said, but Ember was already paddling again for shore. They were almost halfway there.

In a few seconds the dragon had turned again and Justice watched it try another divebomb. Again it blasted fire and again Ember dove to escape the flame.

When the creature saw it had missed its target a second time, it circled back around screeching angrily. Justice tracked it grimly and carefully stood as Ember continued struggling to swim with tiring strokes. The other dragon turned and made a closer dive, hoping to grab at Ember with his claws. Justice waited until just the right moment as it passed over, and then leapt up and touched the dragon's scales.

Instantly the creature cried out in fiery pain and lunged to the side, losing its balance. Justice watched as it spun out of control, trying to get ahold of itself, before crashing into the sea. It thrashed to the surface a second later, roaring, sputtering, and sending thick ripples out across the water.

Justice turned forward and found that Ember had nearly reached the shore, although now he was so exhausted that he struggled to stay afloat.

Keep it up, Justice whispered. *You can do it; just a little bit farther.*

Ember kept paddling for all he was worth. Behind them, the other dragon also floundered in the water, trying to swim after them and make it to shore.

Ember reached it first. He was nearly ready to drop as he pulled himself onto the sand, but he managed to turn around and watch the other dragon approach. Justice dropped to his side, knowing that they were no condition to fight. But then the other dragon did a curious thing. Instead of making for land, it shrank back and roared in frustration at them as it splashed in the water. It made several attempts to come closer, but then always turned back out.

Why doesn't it attack? asked Justice with amazement.

We have the higher ground. It knows better than to fight another of its own kind while still in the water.

Justice watched as the beast began swimming to a spot farther down shore, but when Ember turned as though to follow, it shrank back again, screeched angrily, and then turned around altogether, making for the southern bank across the cove.

But I don't understand, said Justice as he watched it go. *You're exhausted and it can fly. Why does it not fight us, even despite our tactical advantage?*

Perhaps he is afraid of you, said Ember with a weak smile. *But at any rate, it would be a closer match than you think. Dragons become rather helpless when wet; they get waterlogged, then they are unable to breathe fire for several hours and cannot fly until their wings dry out.*

Justice looked at him in surprise, and then he smiled. *Oh; so is this the reason you dislike water?*

Ember looked at him sheepishly and then turned inland. *Well,* he said, *I would admit that I never had much incentive to practice swimming.*

Justice smiled more and followed him across the sand.

Soon the two of them made it to the tree line and Justice found a sheltered place for camp. "I doubt that they will find us today. They will likely assume that we moved on and could be anywhere. Still all the same, it would be better if we traveled at night. You can go ahead and rest until the sun sets."

Ember nodded gratefully and lay down with his back against two trees. Justice started a fire to dry off, and Ember soon fell asleep. Justice let him rest all day as he kept watch. He knew that they only had four days left, but he did not trouble Ember with it. He had earned the respite. Justice sat down against a tree and smiled at the sleeping dragon.

Ember had chosen him.

***

That evening they set out again. Justice kept a close watch on the skies for any of Deception's dragons, but he saw nothing—only a moon that told of the three nights they had remaining to travel. Ember had gotten a decent amount of rest, but had still been awakened by dreams. Justice helped him through the torrents of longing when he needed it, and then left him to fall back asleep.

Now however they were on the move. Time was running out, and Ember knew it well from his Rider's thoughts. He could also feel the strange burden that Justice seemed to always be pondering indirectly, as if to keep it hidden. At one point Ember asked him what the problem was, but Justice only told him not to worry then ceased to think about it altogether.

Eventually they stopped after the night had been mostly spent. Ember settled down, but he noticed that Justice did not make a fire.

Are you afraid that we will be found? he asked.

Justice looked at him and smiled faintly. *No, not tonight my friend. I wonder though what will happen in the morning. Where can you hide all day?*

Ember nodded, but since he did not have any suggestions, he did not say anything.

After a few moments however, he broke the silence in a weak voice. *I think I'm ready now.*

Justice looked up at him. *For what?*

For your fire. I want you to purge me of Deception's influence as much as you can.

Why now? Justice asked, rising to his feet.

Because Deception nearly had me; I could feel it in myself and I don't want to risk being taken again.

Justice nodded. *Then stand here.*

Ember slowly got up and walked over to him. Justice held out his hand and Ember gingerly lowered his head, fear causing him to tremble.

I am afraid of this. Can you offer me no comfort?

Only that afterward my anger will burn less fiercely toward you. Are you ready?

Ember did not say anything, but he did not back away either.

Then try and hold still; look me in the eyes if you can.

Ember did so, and Justice placed his hand on the beast's muzzle.

Instantly fire and searing pain flashed across the dragon's range of vision. He cried and shrieked, but he held his head still as the fire ate deeper into him, burning him to his core. It seemed to be every possible agony at once. Ember felt as though liquid flame now ran through his veins, flowed through every inch of him, made every nerve stand on end.

He felt as though he could not breathe, as though the pain would kill him—and indeed it seemed to be doing so in part. He felt as if a portion of his innermost being was being burned away. Desperately he tried to pull away, to steal relief against the iron that seared his soul.

Then he looked into Justice's face and saw that he was watching him. His master's eyes were pointed, focused, wrathful, and yet somehow kind at the same time. Suddenly Ember knew that Justice still had his Link, that he felt every wave of throbbing pain that pulsed through the dragon's body with each heartbeat. He saw that his Rider knew his agony, that he was enduring it with him, and that he was willing to push through it.

Gradually, Ember forced his mind to concentrate on his master's face, to stare with just as much focus into his eyes. And with it he gained, not a comfort, but a grim determination to hold on, to thrust through each pulse of fire. He anchored his attention on Justice's eyes and held fast to his gaze as wave after wave washed over him and crashed against his soul. The torture was still immense, but he allowed only one thought to enter his mind, and that was of his Rider. Their focus seemed to become one, and Ember felt himself determined to hold out as long as his Rider did, as long as there was still deception within him.

Then slowly the pain began to decrease, and Ember nearly went weak with relief as Justice's hand began to sting less. Still he held on, and still Justice burned, but now his master wore a smile on his face. The fire grew less and less until soon it was nothing but a dull throb, like the heat of a fading coal. Justice released Ember and the dragon fell to the ground, completely exhausted from the endeavor.

"You were brave," said Justice quietly. "You were braver than any creature I have ever seen."

Ember slowly regained his feet, his body still tingling with the effects of the pain. *Did it work?* he asked weakly.

Justice nodded. "I have done all I can do. Your longings should be less powerful now, though you still must fight them. Never let your guard down, or they may spring back up just as powerful as before. If you continue to fight however, and if you hold fast to me, I believe that they will decrease."

Ember nodded without saying anything, and Justice gently stroked his scales for the first time. His hand still stung, but now it was bearable.

Will you ever feel like Peace once did? Will I reach the point where your touch brings comfort instead of pain?

"You have already reached that point," said Justice. "But any pleasure you might receive by my hand would be my gift to you, and I do not think it wise for you to grow reliant upon it again, even from me."

So will I never again enjoy the touch of my Rider?

Justice smiled. *Oh Ember, Ember. Don't worry so much about that. Let my pain keep you in your right mind; follow me because you love me, not because of what I give you.*

I will try, my Eldar.

***

That night Ember at last slept peacefully, waking well into the next day. When he awoke, he saw Justice nearby starting a fire and holding an armful of some type of weed. He seemed genuinely pleased.

"Ember, look what I found!" he said, holding up the plants. "I found a river near the sea, and the bleeding plant grew all along it. We can use it to make a dye."

A dye? said Ember curiously, getting up. *A dye for what?*

"For your scales, to change their color."

The dragon shook his head in disbelief. *You want to change the color I am?*

"Yes, as a disguise. You won't be recognized as easily then."

But I prefer being green, said Ember, almost childishly, as he backed up a step. *It's who I am ever since my birth.*

"But if we could disguise you like this, then any scouts Deception has looking for you wouldn't think twice. There are plenty of other dragons in this country; he might not even recognize you if you both stood face-to-face."

You really think Deception wouldn't recognize me just because I was a different color?

"You'd be surprised how much dragons are identified by their color, and many of you even have similar faces. If Deception saw you, part of him might think you looked familiar, but he would never consider it seriously. Your other most telling attribute is your torn wing, and as long as you keep it hidden you may be able to go undetected from all our enemies."

Ember stepped forward hesitantly. *Are you sure we have to do this? Do we even have time?*

"We don't have time *not* to," said Justice with a smile. "Now get over here and stop cowering."

Ember obeyed and watched as Justice hollowed out a wooden bowl with his dagger and used it to steep the plant in water, creating a dark purple liquid. When Justice began to apply the dye to his scales however, it turned out a cloudy shade of blue. Ember lay still upon the ground as Justice worked rather blissfully all morning until he had painted his dragon from claw to tail. When he finished, Ember stood and tried to get a look at himself. Every scale on his body was now blue all along his back, up his neck, and down his legs.

Ember eyed them distastefully. *Are you sure this will work?*

"It's certainly more likely to work than if we hadn't done anything."

Ember turned back to him. *Tell me, does it wash off?*

Justice laughed a hearty laugh and slapped Ember's flank as he mounted. "Stop worrying so much. No, water will not affect it—although it can be easily burned away with fire. It won't be permanent."

Ember nodded and began to head north through the trees. *Do you like me better as this color?*

Justice laughed again. "No, of course I preferred you when you were green. But it really doesn't matter much to me what shade you are. Had we been ruling over Tarenthia, I might have changed your color weekly just to mess with people. The kingdoms would have been so confused."

Ember smiled slightly at the idea, but then his happiness faded. *If they ruled Tarenthia.* He sighed and continued on without saying anything.

They traveled well into the night without incident before finding a small clearing to stop and rest. For the first time since his imprisonment, Ember dreamed of Peace. He dreamed that the two of them were together again and flying over the plains and forests of Tarenthia. He dreamed that he felt the comforting touch of his Rider, and that they laughed and talked like old friends alone in the airy heights. He dreamed that his soul was at ease within him, that there was not the forbidding thought of death looming in the future; there was only the two of them, as in the days before evil had corrupted their lives.

Ember woke from his sleep into the stillness of night. All around him the trees were calm, and the darkness was peaceful. He felt a throb in his chest as remorse washed over him. That had been his Rider; that could have been his life. But instead he had killed him and now he had brought this fate upon himself. His pain, his wing, his approaching death—all were his own doing.

Ember shifted slightly on the ground and mourned quietly by himself, a tear falling from his eye. Then from somewhere there came the echoing throb of sympathy. Ember slowly turned and saw Justice beside him, his hand resting on his neck. The Rider was lost in a sort of sadness of his own as he stared out blankly into the darkness and stroked the scales of his dragon. His touch, for the first time, was soothing.

He was quietly humming a melody with a melancholy tune, and Ember listened in silence, drinking in the presence of his Rider and trying to understand the lyrics that slowly crossed his mind. When he finished, Justice lay back against a tree and continued to stroke Ember, his touch still offering its calming sympathy.

That was a very beautiful song; what do the words mean?

Justice turned his head ever so slightly to look at him. *It is an old ballad; it speaks of two men that stand on a shore and look out across a forbidden sea. One of them chooses to set sail and explore the unknown while the other begs him to stay in the harbor. But he leaves anyway, and the last line is a prayer from the one who stayed, wishing his friend protection and begging that he might return safely.*

And do you like this song? asked Ember. It was sad, and he wished to hear it again and again.

Justice smiled softly. *Yes; as I child I loved it because it told the danger of striking out upon the sea of morality and leaving the safety of the limits placed upon us. There was one part however that I never understood.*

What part was that?

Justice sighed and sat up straighter, removing his hand. Ember felt the comfort from it fade but didn't say anything.

It never made sense to me why the person who remained prayed for the safety of his friend. As a boy, and even in my later years, I had always believed that the one who left deserved his fate, and it seemed so wrong to wish it otherwise against the cause of justice. He looked at Ember and smiled sadly. *But I think I finally understand it now; love can be a very powerful thing.*

Quietly, he got up and wandered across the clearing through the dark. Ember watched him for a while, then closed his eyes and fell asleep. He never asked Justice if he imparted comfort to him again that night. No dreams troubled him however, and in the days that followed he was disturbed fewer and fewer times by the longings.

They woke at around noon the next day and the two of them set out together one last time. The trees grew thinner as the afternoon progressed, and after a few hours they reached the edge of the forest.

Ahead lay an enormous plain stretching out toward the north and east and ending at the sea to the west.

"We are getting close to it now," said Justice. "There will be no more woods to hinder us. Only one obstacle remains on our way to the battlefield."

Again, Ember felt the strange burden on Justice's mind.

And what obstacle is that?

"You will see shortly; for now, just continue ahead."

Ember took a step forward hesitantly. *Do you think it's safe out there in the open?*

"You should be fine; we won't need to travel for long."

Ember nodded and continued. The plain seemed to stretch out forever, although the gentle hills scattered throughout made it difficult to judge distance. Over one rise and then another they traveled, until at last Ember reached the top of a tall slope where they could see for miles in all directions.

He stopped. Directly ahead of them stretched the outer walls of the largest city—next to Highland itself—that Ember had ever seen. The walls continued far into the distance in either direction, eventually reaching the sea to the west. Behind the walls lay what appeared to be towns and buildings divided by many wide streets and well-paved roads.

What is this place? asked Ember in amazement.

"It is called Sorrow's Pity, and it is by far the largest city in all the Shadowlands. Just to give you an idea, those walls that you see are really only part of a large ring that travels out and around north again to enclose the whole place. In fact, it is Deception's capital; from there, he builds his armies and rules the rest of the kingdoms. It is also where he keeps and trains his dragons."

Why is it called Sorrow's Pity?

Justice turned to his dragon sadly. "Because it is a trap to your kind. You have felt it yourself; sorrow is by no means evil, but because it is the best state in which we can enjoy comfort, many find themselves desiring sadness and pain just to be pitied. Many dragons laden with sorrows, whether by traders or their own will, come to this place longing for comfort and for the hand of Deception to ease their pain. Unfortunately, the soothing of his relief is so pleasant that the dragons decide to stay in their state of sorrow so that they might feel his touch of sympathy again. This place is filled with dragons who are sad, lonely, and burdened with heartache, but who stay so that once a week they might know they are pitied. And the saddest part is many do not even know that is the reason they remain, that their pain is their own making. They waste their lives away in this place and never even realize they are imprisoned by it."

Ember nodded. *I think I understand. A similar thing happened to me when I was first with Deception. Will we need to travel beyond it?*

"Yes, the battlefield my father mentioned lies just outside its northern gates, directly on the other side. But unfortunately, there is no way to travel around this city."

Why not?

"We only have this night and the next before the coming of the full moon, which is not nearly enough time. And besides, the landscape is dotted with small villages and dragon traders who make their living near this place. You would be seen for sure if we traveled for long."

Ember's head fell. *I wish that I could fly you over.*

Justice smiled for just a second. "Very brave of you, but that would be a disaster. The city is miles across, and there would be plenty of skylances and other dragons to bring you down. It seems as though this will be our most challenging barrier."

Then what are we going to do? asked Ember with concern.

"For today, nothing. I'll try and work out a plan by tomorrow. Until then, I think I saw a small cave about half a mile to the east that we can shelter in."

Ember nodded and they turned, traveling down the slope and leaving the expanse of Sorrow's Pity behind.

They found the cave at the bottom of a small rocky ravine that rested between two hills. It was not large, but Ember had room to move about and so he settled down on the dark rocks and let Justice dismount. The two of them said little for the next few hours as the sun descended. Justice paced the cavern from end to end, caught up in thought, while Ember gazed out through the cave entrance at the skies above. He watched as birds flew overhead, as they soared and rode the wind with ease, and a tear slowly came to his eye. He turned away from the opening to watch his Rider. He felt the burden again, and now it weighed heavily upon Justice's mind, though he still seemed to be guarding it within his thoughts.

Tell me, said Ember kindly. *What is it that keeps bothering you? Why won't you tell me?*

Justice stopped and looked at him; he seemed to think about it for a moment.

"It's...nothing. I just need to work through this."

Can't you tell me anything?

Justice sighed. "If you give me your Link, I can tell you a little. I need to know that you aren't listening to my thoughts."

Ember eyed him oddly. *I thought there were supposed to be no secrets between dragon and Rider.*

Justice smiled sadly and leaned back against the cave wall. "In a perfect world yes, but this is not your burden to bear."

Ember nodded and relinquished his Link to his Rider, who put it in his pocket.

"It's about something I need to do," Justice said at last. "Part of me doesn't want to do it, but I know it must be done...I've known it would come to this for quite some time."

And you can't tell me what it is?

"No, I'm afraid that would influence my ability to carry it out." Justice stood and stretched. "I think that I need some fresh air. There is also someone I want to talk to. You stay here for now and wait for my return."

May I have my Link back?

"No, I think I'll hang onto it for now; if you need me though, I will still hear you." He turned to go.

Wait! cried Ember suddenly, and his Rider stopped and looked at him. *I wanted to ask; what Deception said about you, was it really true? Do you really hate what you see in me?*

"Yes, I never lie. It is true that there are things in you that I despise, that I am driven to punish and destroy...though there is less of that in you now than before."

Ember nodded and looked away, signaling that Justice could leave. But his Rider stayed for several more moments, and when Ember looked back he saw that he was fighting the urge to say something.

Finally, Justice choked out: "Ember, do you...do you trust me?"

Of course; I trust you with my life.

A flash of pain seemed to cut across Justice's face, but he only nodded and turned away.

Ember thought he saw a tear in one of his eyes. *Are you all right?* he asked.

"Yes, don't worry about me. Just stay here and remember to keep your wing hidden."

Then he was gone. Ember turned back and moved a little way into the cave before settling down. He could not understand what was wrong with his Rider, and now without his Link he couldn't even feel his presence. He was especially worried that Justice seemed somehow saddened by his trust. Had he said something wrong? Was Justice expecting a different answer? Ember shook his head but remained still. He would ask when he came back.

But Justice was a while in coming back. The sun moved through the final part of its arc and still there was no sign of him. Without his Link, Ember could not even guess how close his Rider was, and so he was forced to wait all alone as evening wore on. Several times Ember called out to Justice, but of course he heard no reply and after a while he stopped. It felt like calling out to a wall.

The sun was nearly set when Ember heard the noise. He jerked his head up and once again heard the sound of pebbles falling, as though someone had bumped the rock wall.

Justice? He called out excitedly. There was no answer.

It felt strange without his Link. Ember was used to having his mind joined with that of another, and to be left alone with the silence of his own thoughts seemed to suffocate him. He desperately looked all around.

Justice, is that you?

He heard the sound of stones shifting again, but there was no answer. Ember strained to see in the dim light. Slowly, he got to his feet.

Instantly there was a cry and suddenly shouts came from everywhere!

Ember stumbled back as the echoes reverberated off the cave walls and overwhelmed his mind. He saw men pouring through the cave opening with torches, and by their light Ember could see that the place was already full of trappers. With a jolt he made for the cave entrance but several of them threw chains over his back and strained against him. He roared and blasted fire but it only seemed to echo everywhere and the men were moving in quick, confusing patterns. He fought hard and struggled with all his might, but he had been caught off guard and this time there was no Rider to help him. With a desperate cry he called out one more time for Justice as the men tried to pull him down, but just as before there was no answer. He was alone.

***

At the top of the hill, Justice watched through the dusk as his dragon was taken by the traders. He fingered the Link in his pocket as the trappers pulled the creature down, muzzled him, and chained his foreclaws together before dragging him out into the open. Justice waited a few more minutes while they fought with the struggling animal to get it onto a transportation cart, and then, without expression, he turned and walked away, a large pouch of money jingling at his side.

The Dragon Trainer

Ember was transported by the traders in a large cage mounted on a cart and pulled by a score of horses. The bars that composed the walls were thick and strong, but he could have melted his way through had his mouth not been muzzled and his legs bound so that he was forced to lay on his side. The journey to Sorrow's Pity was not long, but the dragon hardly noticed. Nor did he realize when they entered through the enormous gate. His heart was crushed and his thoughts at war.

Why had Justice not come? He should have heard his cry; why did he delay? How could he allow his own dragon to be captured? Why did he not chase after the traders now? All these things and more assaulted Ember's mind, but there were darker thoughts as well. How could the traders have found him? Had they seen him from a distance? Why did Justice not know?

*Justice...*Ember growled a barely audible sound. Justice knew where he was; he was the only person who knew where he was. Desperately the dragon tried to stop the train of thought, but now the curiosity and rage pent up within him seemed beyond his control. Justice had a burden. What was he planning to do that he couldn't tell? Who had he left to talk to? He had taken both Links; why would he have done that if not to keep the valuable treasure from being stolen? Ember growled louder, anger rising within him. He had been betrayed!

Of course, it was possible that Justice had simply been late in coming and the traders had happened to find him, but that felt like an unlikely explanation. Why had Justice taken the Link? Why had he seemed hurt when he found he was so deeply trusted? Was it because he knew what he was about to do, and felt guilty?

...there are things in you that I despise, that I am driven to punish and destroy...

...You fool! You will be destroyed! Just wait; he'll betray you the first chance he gets...

So it had finally happened. Justice had released him to his doom. That should have been no surprise. He had promised from the first day to kill him—that he would pay for his treason.

*But not here...*Ember struggled to grasp the thought. Yes, Justice had promised to kill him, but only after they had reached the King. That had been the agreement, and when had Justice ever lied? Ember's rage still burned against his Rider, but now he clung desperately to this last bit of hope. Justice was gone, but he would not abandon Ember. He couldn't, he wouldn't. He had sworn to protect him, to lead him back home if possible. Ember knew his thoughts were wild and desperate, but still he clung against reason and hope to the promise of his Rider—it was all he had left.

It was dusk as the traders pulled his cage down the streets. Ember did not care. He lay quiet, motionless, detached and dead to the world. He was alone. Whether his Rider still cared for him or not, he was alone now. Tears came to the dragon's eyes. Something in the back of his mind warned against sorrow, that it would be dangerous in this place, but he paid it no heed. After all, it had been Justice that said that, and what did he care for him?

Ember felt the cart come to a halt and the men surround him. He ignored them all; his eyes were closed and his body still. He wondered if he would be recognized, if his dyed scales really were the disguise they had seemed. His torn wing lay folded against his left side. No one would see the gash unless he spread it out, and the traders had wrapped a chain around him that would keep him from doing that, even if he wanted. Apparently, they did not yet know he was unable to fly, which meant his identity was likely still a secret...although it certainly would not be for long. Around him, he heard the men saying things in harsh words.

"Why won't the stupid beast move?"

"He's been like that ever since we captured him."

"Is he sick?"

"Bring me that whip; I'll strike the life back into him." Ember heard a swishing sound and then his right wing stung, but still he did not move.

"I don't know what's wrong with him."

"Deception will take care of him, don't worry."

"Why wait for Deception?" asked a voice that sounded cold and hard. "Let me have a chance with him."

"What can you possibly know about dragons, Dark Ranger?"

"I know far more than you would think," the voice barked. "Give me three minutes alone with him and I'll see to it that he livens up."

"Be my guest. You won't make a difference."

"We will see."

Ember heard the sound of footsteps approaching from behind his head as the crowd quieted, but he did not turn. Step-by-step the heavy boots crunched against the ground, getting closer and closer, until they stopped just outside the cage bars. Ember tensed, feeling breath against his neck, but still he did not move. When the ranger spoke, he did so in the softest of whispers.

"Ember..."

Immediately Ember's ears perked up and he turned his head to stare at the man. He wore a black cloak with a hood that cast a shadow across his face, but it was close enough that his features were barely visible.

Justice? said Ember in disbelief. *Is that you?*

"Of course it's me," he said, still whispering so that no one else could hear. "I'm sorry to do this to you; you have no idea the agony I went through, how many times I nearly turned back. But I knew this had to be done; it is the only way through this place."

If I needed to be captured, then why didn't you tell me about it?

"For three reasons. First, I needed the trappers to think they had actually captured their dragon, and you would not have resisted naturally had you known. Second, I didn't want you to have to spend your last few hours not only alone, but also in the fear of anticipation; I wanted you to have peace of mind for as long as possible. But thirdly and most importantly, I needed to test your trust. I needed to see how you would react, even when it seemed like I had betrayed you."

Ember's eyes fell. *I am sorry. I was angry with you; I doubted.*

"Yes, I know," said Justice. "But that was not all I felt in you." He reached his hand through the bars and touched Ember's forehead. His hand stung worse than normal. "You decided to trust me; you did not abandon hope completely. Admittedly I am disappointed you doubted as you did, but you still see yourself as mine, and you will need that if you are to survive in this place."

I am sorry, my Rider. I will try to trust you more.

"I know, and the trial you faced was difficult. Let us make you more prepared for the next one." Justice took a step back and extended his arms slightly, "Do you like my disguise?" he asked.

I do; where did you get it?

"I bought it. Turning you in paid very handsomely; it even earned me a place among the dragon keepers here."

You sold me?

"Of course not! The money I received came merely from telling where you *were*. I was very careful to tell the traders that you were likely owned by someone, and that by taking you, they would bring down the full wrath of your master. They said they knew the risk and that they didn't care. Judgment will come upon them in due time."

Ember smiled at his Rider. *You are very clever, my Eldar.*

Justice grinned. "Thank you; I will make sure to see you tonight. For now though, act lively and make these people here think I'm some miracle worker."

Ember shifted his weight as best he was able to and snarled at the people behind his Rider.

Justice turned around and gestured at the dragon. "See!" he said to the crowd. "He's fine! What did I tell you?"

"Amazing!" cried one of the men. "We could hardly get him to move!"

"You very clearly have a way with dragons."

"You must join our circle of dragon riders; come, I'll make sure you have a spot on the Council." The men led Justice away down the road and

Ember felt his cage jerk into motion again. He saw his Rider turn for just a second and wink at him. Ember nodded in reply and then turned to watch as they traveled down the dusty street.

Not long afterward they arrived at what was called the prison house, although it looked more like a long wooden building than a prison. Ember was brought inside through an enormous doorway bolted with a heavy bar from the outside. The place was all one room, composed of a long, wide space that went from one end to the other. All along one side of the walkway were kept the dragons, each in their own individual cells that reminded Ember a bit of the stalls of a stable. Of course, they were far bigger, enough to hold a large dragon comfortably, and each had a door made of iron bars. But for the most part it seemed more like a place to house the beasts rather than to contain them.

Ember did not fight as he was transferred to an open cage between two other dragons. He was far too exhausted and hungry to bother, and now that he knew Justice was near he wanted to attract as little attention as possible. Once he was in his cell, the traders removed his chains and even his muzzle before locking the door and leaving for the night. This struck Ember as a little odd, because there was nothing then to stop him from breathing fire, but he let it rest. In fact, he almost felt disappointed that they had left him with so much freedom within his cell. Why not keep him chained and muzzled if they were to imprison him at all? If they were going to take away a dragon's freedom, why not go the whole way and make it *look* captured?

Pity. Ember shook his head. That was why he felt disappointed— he wanted to be pitied. Quickly he shook the thoughts away and called silently for Justice.

It was awhile before he came. The hall was dark except for a few sparsely placed lanterns, and the other dragons had all fallen asleep. Ember wouldn't have heard the sound at all had he not been listening—the sound of a door gently shutting. He looked up to see the black-cloaked figure approaching like a silent shadow, and rose softly to greet him.

"Hello, my Ember," Justice whispered.

Hello, my Eldar, Ember replied.

"So, this is where they put you?" he spoke quietly, looking around. "I hope they didn't treat you badly."

No, this place is fine. The cells are actually rather nice.

"Of course they are; they're meant to make dragons feel comfortable here so that they don't wish to leave. It gives them a safe place from which to feel sorrowful."

I understand; I won't mind waiting here though.

"Really? You should. You must never forget what it is like to be free, to soar through the air with your Rider. Don't get too comfortable here."

I will try not. What is the next step in our plan?

"For now, you must lay low while I try to come up with a way out. The night after tomorrow is the full moon, and I have yet to figure out how we will escape to the battlefield before then. But don't worry; I'll find a way. Until then however, keep your wing hidden and don't let anyone know who you are. We will be out of here soon enough."

Ember bowed his head. *Thank you, my Rider.*

"Don't worry," he said, reaching through the bars and touching Ember's muzzle. His hand burned slightly. "I'll take care of everything, I promise."

Could I have my Link back? I desperately need to feel your consciousness again.

"I'm afraid not, my Ember. It would mark you as a Rider's dragon. For now, you will need to draw your strength by speaking to me, even though I cannot reply. This is only temporary, but you must not fall under the comfort of sorrow. It will be nearly impossible for me to revive you in this place if you do."

Ember nodded and lay down drowsily. *I understand. Will you stay with me tonight?*

"For now, until you fall asleep."

I understand, said Ember, yawning. He closed his eyes. *Could you sing me that song again? The one about the sea?*

"Ah, but don't you see what that is? You already desire for me to comfort you. If I do so now, you will long for it more tomorrow."

It's a pity, said Ember. *It was such sad, beautiful song.*

"I know, and that is why we must not sing it here. We'll save it, as a promise. I will make sure you hear it once more before we meet the King."

Ember gave a small nod and in a few more minutes he was asleep, although a tear trickled down his snout.

Justice however did not leave immediately. He stayed, staring at the sleeping form of his dragon, and then began to pace back and forth. He stopped once again to gaze at Ember and then growled, resuming his pacing. Why? Why did it have to be this way? Cursed law! Cursed, cursed law! It made no distinction between the guilty and the repentant, between those who were lost and who could be saved. Why? Why did Ember have to die? Justice shook his head as he paced and fumed to himself. The dragon was getting better; he had been taking great steps toward shaking off Deception's influence, and he would have to die in the end anyway. It seemed so unfair. And yet it was perfectly fair. It was justice.

Justice turned away and shook his fist angrily. "Why? Why, my brother, did you send me to save a creature that could not be saved? You knew the law, that there was nothing I could do; why did you make me promise to try?"

Desperately Justice searched the archives of his memory seeking any loophole, any exemption, anything that could save Ember's life. But there was none. There was no question what treason was, and there was no question of its consequence. Ember's life was forfeit; it had been since the day he killed Peace.

For the first time in his life Justice wished that he had given himself toward some other calling, that he had not devoted his life and soul to following the law. Now he was bound to it. He could not break it; he could not abandon it. To do so would undermine everything he was, would counter his very character. The cause of justice drove him, powered him, thrust him along toward one inevitable end. He would need to kill his own dragon, and there was nothing he could do about it now.

With a slight moan, and then a growl, Justice turned one last time to look at Ember, and then marched out through a side door and into the night.

***

Ember woke at what he took to be early morning, though the prison house had no windows to view the sky. Many of the other dragons had awakened before him, and Ember wondered if they typically slept so lightly in their cells. Despite their presence however, he felt desperately alone. He instinctively searched for Justice, but of course could not find him. It felt oppressive without him there, as if some invisible weight was trying to press its way into his soul. He watched as the other dragons stretched and moved drowsily, mournfully, and couldn't help but feel the heavy presence of sorrow and sadness.

Quickly Ember turned away and crouched on the straw-covered floor of his cell, staring through the bars of his doorway at the wooden wall across from him. Silently he started to speak to Justice. It felt strange at first to talk into the nothingness, but he reassured himself that Justice was in range, that he would hear, and spoke more earnestly. He told of what the morning was like, of how he missed his Rider, of the sorrow of the other dragons, of the hope he had to escape and be reunited.

He spoke what was on his mind and poured it out like a prayer, the knowledge that Justice was listening keeping him sane.

Eventually he finished talking and stood up. He wondered if Justice really had been nearby to hear him. He felt a little silly at the thought that maybe he had only been talking to a wall, and so he sat back and looked around. There was nothing to do aside from keeping his wing hidden, so Ember tried talking to the dragons on either side of him. The one to his left was a light green female named Misery, and she was a very sour-tempered beast. Mostly she kept to herself, and when she spoke at all it was as if she was snapping in annoyance. Apparently she was angry with her surroundings as well as sorrowful, and desired to talk to no one except Deception. Ember quickly gave up trying to communicate with her.

The dragon on his right, however, was a bit friendlier. He was a deep blue creature called Fearful, but while he seemed willing to talk he was also very timid and would often keep to himself. He spent most of his time curled up on the ground and moaning softly, apparently caught up in the memories of a painful past.

When Ember spoke to him, he did so tentatively. "How long have you been here?"

"I don't know," Fearful said quietly, staring out ahead through his cage bars from where he lay on the ground. "Maybe a year or two. It's hard to say."

"What do you do most of the time?" asked Ember curiously. From what he could see, most of the other dragons seemed slow and not at all ambitious.

"Eat, sleep, not much else," snorted Fearful with a small smile, which then quickly disappeared. "About once a week Deception comes by to see each of us, and sometimes he takes us out on missions, but aside from that there isn't much to do. Not that I would want anything else; I prefer to be here alone, away from the noise and the cruelty of men."

For some reason, Ember took pity on him, though he wondered if he should.

"But not all men are bad," Ember said. "Isn't there anything at all in this place that brings you joy?"

"Well," said Fearful slowly, quietly, "There is the Dragon Trainer."

"Who's that?" asked Ember.

"He's just some old man," snapped Misery from his left. "He comes by here every day or two to make sure we can still fly under one of the riders. Fearful is one of his favorites and he gives him special treatment."

"He does not!" said Fearful starting up, though still not daring to raise his voice much above a whisper. "He has many dragons to care for; he doesn't have much time for me." He lay back down. "Still though, he seems to be the only person here who cares."

"You whimpering little wretch!" huffed Misery. "That's only because you're too afraid to approach any other human you see! You ought to stop acting so hurt and broken just to attract his attention."

"Who is the Dragon Trainer?" asked Ember with curiosity and a little apprehension.

"His name is Guidance," said Fearful, turning away from Misery and back toward the wall. "You'll see him soon. He's scheduled to come this morning."

Ember nodded.

They didn't have to wait long. Less than half an hour later Ember heard the great doors opening and looked up to see the Dragon Trainer enter with an escort of five soldiers. Ember wasn't sure what he had been expecting, but for some reason the man took him completely off guard. He was rather old, maybe close to sixty, and slightly fat. His stride however was calm and sure, and he strode from one cage to another as though he came there every day. Several of the dragons rose to meet him, but many hardly seemed to notice. A few even growled softly. Guidance didn't care, however. He started at the far end of the line and worked his way up, speaking with each dragon individually and making notes on a piece of paper he held in his hand. He called each dragon by name, even those that snarled at him, and indeed seemed so caught up in his work and one-sided conversations that he was hardly aware of the guard escort around him.

Ember waited nervously for the man to make his way up to him. He seemed nice enough, but if there was one person who might figure out his secret, it would likely be him. Silently he communicated to Justice everything he saw, hoping he would be nearby if things went bad.

Eventually, Guidance made his way up the aisle until he was at Fearful's cage. The dragon gingerly got up and moved closer to him, allowing the man to stroke his muzzle through the bars.

"There, there," the man said. "I know; I miss you too." He did seem to talk a little softer and a little more sincerely to Fearful that to the other dragons.

Fearful closed his eyes and nuzzled his hand gently, a tear in his eye.

"I know, I know; you want to fly again. But you already went up yesterday and I can't take you again until tomorrow. There are some that haven't gone in nearly a week."

Fearful made a small whimpering sound.

"Shh," said the trainer gently. "I'll come back soon for you, I promise."

He backed away slowly and the blue dragon stared at him sadly for a few moments before turning away. There was a pause for a few seconds as the man wrote something down, and then he moved on to Ember's cage.

"Ahh! What have we here? A new one?" he said when he looked up.

He turned to the guards. "Take the first three out for some flight training. I prefer to be alone when I get to know a new dragon."

The men obeyed immediately and moved back down the line where they unlocked several of the far cages and led their dragons out through the main entrance. When they had closed the great doors behind them, the Dragon Trainer turned back to Ember.

"Now I can talk to you alone," he said good-naturedly. He wrote something down on his paper. "You're a beautiful one, aren't you? I wonder if you have a name."

Ember eyed him cautiously. The man still made him nervous, despite how nice he seemed.

"I ought to take you out for a flight and see how well you do," said the old man. "How would you like that?"

Instantly Ember shrunk back, folding his wings more tightly against his sides.

Guidance seemed surprised. "Don't you like to fly?" he asked.

Secretly, Ember began to call for Justice, hoping that he would stand nearby if nothing else.

"Nearly all dragons love to fly," said the trainer thoughtfully. "It's about the only thing any of them seem to enjoy in this place."

Ember continued to back away from the door, adding a whimper for good measure.

"It's all right! It's all right!" said Guidance kindly, writing something else down on his paper. "We don't have to go out today, though we will need to eventually. I can give you some time to settle in. No doubt this seems like a strange place to you. Come closer; let me get a good look at you."

Still Ember shrunk back.

"You'll be all right; I promise I won't hurt you," said the man good-naturedly.

Slowly Ember began to come forward. The trainer reached his hand through the iron bars and Ember tentatively let him touch his muzzle. He tensed for some emotional burst from the man, but there was nothing. Apparently, only Deception knew that trick—probably to maintain control.

"Ahh, what a nice blue you are," he said kindly, letting his hand run back and forth across the dragon's cold scales. "You don't shimmer as you ought to though. It's a pity the light doesn't reflect more brightly. It's almost as if there were a film clouding your scales."

Immediately Ember's mind jolted though he tried not to show it. Carefully he tried to back away, calling for Justice and hoping that the trainer wouldn't become suspicious.

But he did.

"That's strange. It's almost as if someone dyed you a different color," Guidance said, looking at him thoughtfully. "Yes, now that I think about it, that's exactly what it felt like. Poor creature. Couldn't your masters live with you in your natural state? I wonder how you used to look."

Desperately Ember called out for his Rider. *Where could he be?*

"Judging by your shade, I would guess that you might have been a hue of green once, perhaps like an emerald."

Suddenly the man stopped, as if his words had turned to snakes in midair. He stared at Ember with his eyes wide, his mouth open. "You've been dyed from green to blue," he glanced at his left wing, "And you're afraid to fly."

He looked Ember directly in the eyes. The dragon stared back. "You're...you're the one he's looking for, the one called Ember!"

Ember growled and instinctively tried to blow fire, but nothing came out except for smoke. The Dragon Trainer began to back up more quickly. "But if you're here...then...then where's your Rider? Is he with you?"

Ember growled, not sure what else to do, and several of the other dragons started to take notice.

Guidance began to back toward the door. "He must be nearby! I must go; I must tell Deception!" And with that he turned and ran for the exit.

Ember roared after him, but the man did not stop until he reached the door and flung it open.

There he found himself staring directly into the eyes of a figure cloaked in black.

Immediately the Dragon Trainer started to back up. "Dark Ranger! I didn't...are you—"

"What has happened here?" said the figure, advancing smoothly as the door shut behind him. "My dragon was distressed; he called for me. What have you done?"

The man fumbled as he continued trying to edge away down the hall. "Justice? Are you—? I promise, I meant no harm..."

"That is not what Ember believes," said Justice coldly. "You discovered our secret. You were leaving to tell Deception, were you not?"

"I...I..."

"Were you not?" roared Justice.

Several of the dragons looked up lazily, but they seemed strangely passive.

"Yes," gulped Guidance.

"Then you must die," said Justice, reaching into the folds of his cloak for his katana.

"Please!" cried the man, stumbling as he continued to retreat. He was nearing the end of the hall. "Please! I don't mean any harm! I won't tell; I swear!"

"I have no way of trusting you. You are a servant of Deception, and I cannot risk our safety. Your death will be made to look like an accident. Our secret will die with you."

"But I have a family!" cried Guidance. His back was almost against the wall. "I have a wife and children, and there are dragons here I have loved..."

"It matters not. Everyone here will be dead within two days when the King strikes. If you have loved ones, you should have thought of that before you took up living here."

He raised his katana high as Ember watched. Beside him, Fearful leapt to his feet. The sword came down and Guidance leapt back to avoid the stroke. He stumbled and fell on his back; Justice was immediately on top of him.

"Please—I beg you—don't kill me!"

"Give me one reason why I should not," growled Justice. "Your association with the enemy warrants your death."

"I know! I'm sorry! I swear I will not tell anyone."

"It is too late for that," Justice said, raising his sword above his head. Fearful gave a cry; Misery also watched spellbound with horror.

Justice; please.

Justice stopped and turned to see Ember watching him, concern and fear filling his eyes. He looked back to the man he was about to kill, and for just a second he saw his own dragon's eyes reflected in his, begging for mercy, the mercy he could not give. The mercy Ember could never receive.

For several moments Justice stayed there, poised to strike, knowing that the man before him held the power to destroy everything if released. Then he slowly lowered his sword.

"You swear not to tell?"

"I swear. I promise you that none shall learn of your presence."

Justice stared at him for several more moments, eyes flaming. Then he slowly got up. "Then get out of here. Don't let me see you again."

Immediately the old man got up shakily, edged around Justice, and ran to the door. Justice stayed a moment as he watched him go, then gave a brief look at Ember before quickly striding out of the building as well. The tension in the room seemed to die as the door slammed. Ember sank to the ground, feeling strangely exhausted.

Beside him, he heard Misery say, with a little amazement: "Who was that?"

Ember snorted slightly. "He's my Rider."

Fearful looked at him with wide eyes. "That man is with you?" he said in a quaking voice. "Aren't you terrified of him?"

"No; I trust him with my life."

"Don't be so sure of yourself just because you're with a dangerous man," warned Misery sourly. "He seems like the type that might decide someday just to kill you on a whim!"

"He has already decided to kill me."

That brought a silence to the dragons on both sides of him. Ember didn't look at either, however. He stared instead through his prison bars blankly at the wall in front of him.

"If he is going to kill you, then why do you still follow him?" he heard Fearful ask. "You could escape him easily here; you could be free."

Ember snorted. "I don't wish to leave him. True, he is violent and dangerous, but I follow him still because...because that is who I am. I need to follow, it is my nature—and I was never happier than in the days when I served a Rider, when I served Peace."

"You mean enslaved to a Rider!" growled Misery. "Don't think that I don't know what it's like to have one; at least here, the humans leave us alone for much of the time."

"What did you like about Peace?" asked Fearful with curiosity. "You say his name as though he were different. What was it like for him to be your Rider?"

Ember smiled sadly and lay down. He stared forward, trying to recall his memories, and began: "I remember the days of my former master. They are distant and cold—buried by time, heartache, and pain—but I will never forget what they were like..."

And so he told the story of his old Rider, of what it had been like, of the love and freedom he had held. He told of his mistakes, heartbreaks, and sorrows, and oddly enough both dragons listened. When he finally reached the end, he fell silent, the memories still floating around him like wisps of smoke. He waited to hear what his companions would say, but deep in his heart he knew Justice had heard his every word and that was enough. Beside him, he heard Misery huff.

"I'll tell you what you are: you are a fool. Your mind has been so twisted by your masters that you no longer even understand what you say. You were conditioned to serve a Rider; all of us were. But I retain a grip on what I really am, and that is a dragon. You and the others here are not worthy to be called that anymore."

She turned away and lay down on the floor of her cell. Ember looked at Fearful to see what he would say, but he remained silent, apparently lost in thought.

***

"You are late, Dark Ranger!"

It was late evening, and the Council was already settled around the table when the black-cloaked figure entered through the doors. The leader eyed him sharply. "Did you not know what time we would be meeting?"

"Yes, I did," he said as he took his seat. "Unfortunately, I was delayed. What have you been discussing?"

"There has been a disagreement as to when we should mount our attack. Deception could not be here today, but he charged us with choosing when we should prepare the dragons for our final battle against Highland."

The cloaked figure seemed surprised. "The dragons here will be in the attack? Tell me, how many of them?"

"All of them. For reasons we cannot understand, Deception seems to fear defeat."

"So even the dragons that were brought here only yesterday will be flown in?"

"Yes, though the newer ones will be behind the main charge. You may even be allowed to ride one of them."

The figure was silent for a moment. At last he asked: "And when do you plan on doing this?"

"That's exactly what we cannot decide. Some feel we should do it the day after tomorrow, before the full moon and before the King can strengthen his position. Others say we should wait and take more time to prepare. What advice do you have?"

The figure was silent a little while longer. Finally, he said: "I can only offer you this: if Highland attacks you first, you will almost certainly be crushed. I think that your best hope will be to attack while you still have the time to prepare your army. I would not delay; you should move before the full moon if possible."

The others around the table were silent.

Finally, the leader stood. "And are you sure of your judgment? Will Highland destroy us if we wait?"

"Trust me," said the figure. "I know more about that nation than you'd think."

****

The following morning Deception walked leisurely atop the town's wall in the early light. Just beyond the northern gate the King's army was camped across the battlefield, lending a suspended tension to the air. Deception was nervous. This was the end of his plan; he had summoned his forces together and now all he had to do was kill the King and Highland would be his!

But somehow, he felt strangely hesitant. If only he had destroyed the Dragon Rider Pact. If only Ember did not still live. But the King would die; it would all come to nothing. Deception grunted to himself, wishing he felt as sure of himself now as he once had all those years ago.

When Deception had first fled Highland, he had come to the Shadowlands to be hidden while he formed his plan. Oh, the years he

had spent traveling from kingdom to kingdom searching for the Curse. But everywhere he went, he also told the secret to taming dragons. Every town he visited soon began to prepare their dragon eggs, to raise up hatchlings of their own to extend their power. The fools! Never did they realize they were training his army!

Soon after the King had settled down far away in Highland to train the next Rider, Deception had risen up. It had only taken a few rightly placed words to gain power: a promise here, an alliance there. Soon everyone was united with him, and then under him. Some kings resisted, but he did not fear them.

And of course, the dragons were his. He alone knew how to impart emotion to them, and so they all flocked under his care. Soon he had managed to unite every nation together, and soon after that he was their sole leader. For many years he had sent the dragon trappers out to find all the domestic dragons raised by private families, and now they served him. This place was his kingdom. From it he had mustered the strength to challenge Highland, and now the final battle would soon be complete!

And yet he still feared...

To his side he heard the crunch of boots as a man approached. He turned as the man saluted him.

"The Council has reached a decision," he said. "We will attack to-morrow morning."

Deception eyed him oddly. "Before the full moon? What made you decide on that?"

"It was divided, but there was one who made a persuasive argument."

"And who was this person?"

"He calls himself the Dark Ranger."

"The one who arrived here yesterday?" said Deception with surprise. "Interesting."

He turned away, a hope suddenly beginning to rise within him. "Tell me, there haven't been any new dragons brought in recently have there? Perhaps at the same time he arrived?"

"I think a few. Why?"

Deception smiled. "Oh, nothing. We shall attack tomorrow if that is your decision. Before we go however, I want to visit each of my dragons one last time. Schedule it for tonight, and..."

"And what, my lord?"

"And have the Dark Ranger accompany me. I want him to watch as I touch each of my precious beasts."

6

The Final Night

Justice rounded the corner of the prison house and sank to the ground, strangely exhausted. He was hidden, but through the early light of morning he could still keep an eye on the door in case Ember needed him. But Ember would be all right now. Justice smiled wearily. He had done it! It was a shaky arrangement, but everything would work out. On the day of the attack he would be Ember's rider, and in the commotion of the fight no one would notice as he led Ember around the battlefield to behind the King's army. They would be safe, and they would make it before the full moon. All would be well.

He heard a sound behind him and then a voice that whispered: "Dark Ranger; please forgive me, but I must speak with you."

Justice spun around in surprise, and then growled. "I thought I said to make sure I never saw you again."

Guidance took a step back, but then continued, speaking firmly. "I wanted to thank you for sparing my life. I have served Deception ever since he first came here and he told us frightening stories about

Highland; he said that you were cruel, that you enslaved, that you killed without mercy. For the longest time I believed him, as did everyone else. But when you let me go, even when I could have told Deception about Ember, that woke me up. It showed me that what Deception told us was a lie, that maybe you and your kingdom can be trusted."

"So, what do you want from me?"

"I want to live!" said Guidance, throwing his arms out. "I want to join you and have my family escape this coming destruction! What must I do to avoid the King's wrath?"

"You must leave, and before tonight. Escape from here while you can, and when the battle is over, come quickly to the King and beg his mercy."

"You expect he will win?"

"I know he will win—and I think in his heart, Deception knows it too."

"Then thank you—thank you for giving me another chance!" said Guidance. "Now I want to help you if I can. I want to make sure that you and Ember get out of here safely."

"There is nothing you can do, aside from keeping quiet about our identities."

"But I can help! I know much; I think I can be of service."

"How could you possibly help us?"

"Your dragon has a torn wing," Guidance pointed out. "I could fix it."

Justice turned to him in surprise. "What? You could fix his wing? How is that possible?"

"I think I could sew it back together like one would a ship's sail."

"Would that work? Would he be able to fly again?"

"I have only performed the procedure twice before, but each of those times it has worked."

"When can you do this?"

"I could have it done as soon as this afternoon. I will need a team of six men, but we can finish in under an hour."

"But wouldn't your men see the tear in his wing and realize who he is?"

"Deception has not told everybody the description of the dragon he seeks. I will be sure to pick those of my men who are slow-witted; they will not guess your secret."

Justice smiled, though a little sadly. "Then do it. I have long felt the desire in Ember to fly once again. It will be the last gift I can give him."

***

Ember quickly agreed to the procedure, though he moved nervously as he was led out of the prison house and into another building used for treating dragons. Justice followed closely as Guidance and his six men brought him into a spacious room cut off from the rest of the building.

After strapping the dragon down, Guidance proceeded to direct his men as they carefully unfolded the injured wing and began to stitch the torn part back together using a thin leather strip as a thread. Ember winced each time they pulled the needle through his wing, but he held on, keeping his eyes on Justice and imagining what it would be like to soar through the air again.

As the men finished, Guidance stood close by Justice and said to him, "I believe the process has worked. Your dragon behaved marvelously. Of course, if we had more time, I would have cut the edges of his wing so that they could be joined together to heal as one, making the fix permanent. I might still later if we all make it through this."

Justice laughed sadly. "Thank you for your help, though I doubt we will be coming back. Would he have been able to fly normally for the rest of his life?"

"Yes, I believe so. Of course, the scar would remain, and his wing would feel different than the other when he folded it against his side, but aside from that he should have been just as any other dragon."

Across the room, the men finished with Ember and began to pack up their supplies. "You know," said Guidance, "I could use someone to fly him, to test his wing. Would you be available this evening?"

At his words, Ember quickly looked toward his Rider, his eyes glowing with excitement.

Justice smiled. "It would be my honor, Dragon Trainer."

That evening Ember was led out again, this time to a flat grassy area outside the city walls. The night was clear and warm; above, the faint stars poked through the sky in the dying light of the sunset, and the moon—one night from full—seemed to sail through their midst. Guidance led him, along with the Rider, out to a large clearing where the sky was wide open and inviting above them. Of course, there were still other men with them, as Guidance was not allowed to take a dragon out without supervision.

When they got to the center, Guidance stopped and said to Ember: "All right, here we are. This is your first flight, so be careful and don't travel too high. Your wing won't fully heal until tomorrow, so don't put too much strain on it." He smiled and, leaning closer to the dragon, whispered: "And please don't fly too far away. If anyone thinks you are trying to escape, they'll send up other dragons to intercept you."

Ember nodded and Guidance smiled again before stepping back.

Ember turned his head toward Justice. *I do not believe we have flown together since the day we stormed Watergate.*

"I think you're right," Justice whispered. He stroked his dragon's snout, and his hand burned slightly. "Are you ready to go up?"

You have no idea how long I have been waiting for this.

"Oh, I can feel it, my friend."

Justice mounted and Ember slowly stretched his wings, something he had been unable to do freely since they first entered Sorrow's Pity. He moved them gently, feeling the resistance of the air against them, and then pushed off from the ground with his hind legs. They launched into the air and Ember continued to carefully beat his wings at a consistent pace so they rose slowly. Pure joy hummed through him.

Upon his back, Justice held on as they began to rise higher and as the ground became distant so that Guidance was hard to see. "That's far enough," he said gently, and drew forth from his cloak Ember's Link, which he threw around the dragon's neck.

Ember held his wings steady and they began to glide.

I had no idea how much I missed this, said Ember in a sad tone. *I had longed so much to soar amidst the clouds again.*

Justice nodded. *Bank to your right,* he said. *You don't want to make them think we are trying to escape.*

Ember obeyed and began to circle the clearing.

What did you like so much about flying? asked Justice. *I would think that it would get tiring.*

Oh, it was, said Ember. *In fact, it is a bit even now because I'm so out of practice. It took me nearly two years before I had the endurance to fly all day with Peace. But how I loved it! When we were in the air, it was just the two of us. We were alone, and I was helping him to keep the nations at peace with one another. It was so calm up there; I had no fears, no worries. I knew that what I did was right and was not confused by the emotions and temptations on the ground. I was where I belonged.*

They continued to fly in silence for a while longer as Ember began to slowly circle downward. *I do wish that we could go farther,* he said longingly. *I want to dive and spin and dart through the clouds at full speed.*

Justice laughed. *Oh, don't worry. We will have plenty of that tomorrow when we break off and head toward the safety of Highland's army.*

Yes, I look forward to that.

Justice smiled again, but sadly.

Ember sensed it. *You seem worried,* he said.

That is because I learned something that is to happen tonight, said Justice. *Every week or so, Deception comes around to each of his dragons and touches them, pitying them so that they desire to stay. He has decided to do so again tonight, and he wants me to be with him.*

Why?

I believe he suspects us and wants to watch my reaction to find out which of his dragons you are. For now I think he is still unsure, but if you fall to him then both of our identities will be revealed.

But won't your face give you away? And won't he also be able to tell I am disguised, like Guidance did?

Do not worry; the old Dragon Trainer says he has some oil that will make your scales glimmer like they should, and he has also found a way to paint my face so that I will be unrecognizable. We should be all right unless he breaks into you.

But if that happens, you can just overcome him, couldn't you?

I am certainly willing to die trying, but even if I succeeded all would be lost. I wouldn't be able to disguise his death as an accident and they will not lead the charge without him. You must not let him take you; you must resist.

I will do so with all heart.

I hope so, my dear Ember, I hope so.

They continued to fly lower, in a few minutes they would be on the ground again.

Justice, said Ember hesitantly after a few moments. *What will become of all the other dragons? There are some that may be willing to turn.*

Justice was silent for a few seconds. *I'm afraid they will all be killed when Highland invades. I cannot ride more than one.*

Still, could not something be done? I wish they could be given another chance.

I know. I will see what I can do.

As they neared the clearing's grassy floor, Justice quickly unfastened Ember's Link and stowed it within his cloak. "I'm sorry," he whispered. "I'll give it back tomorrow when we flee together."

With a small rumble, the dragon touched down on the ground and Justice jumped down from his back.

"He flies well," he said to Guidance with a wink.

Guidance nodded and turned to the men with him. "All right then, take him back."

They quickly began to lead the dragon away, though Ember gave one last look behind him as they parted.

"He behaves so well!" said Guidance as he watched them go. "He does not fight them, and I have not seen such joy in a dragon's eyes for years. None of the others seem to enjoy flying as much as he."

"That is because Ember has hope, and he has not surrendered himself to sorrow."

"Is that what you think the others have done?" asked Guidance as they started back.

"Yes," said Justice "They long to be pitied, to have someone come and lay their hands on them compassionately. You likely only contribute to the problem by acting sympathetic."

"But I *do* pity them! I want to see them thrive and enjoy life, though none seem to be able to do so in this place."

"If you want to help them, you might start by laying off the sympathy and giving them some tough love."

"Tell me, do you not pity these poor creatures at all?"

Justice stopped and thought about it for a moment. "I do not pity them for their pain, as they bring it upon themselves. What I do pity is that they live in deception, that they don't even realize what they are doing to themselves."

"Could you help them? There is one in particular I love; he is kept in the cell next to Ember. For so long I have wished to see him thrive, to be happy. I feel that he could become a great creature if he did, but he seems lost in a perpetual state of despair and I am unable to reach him."

"There is only one thing I can do, and it is painful. It took Ember a while before he agreed to it and I am not sure if your dragon would be willing."

"Then ask him. Please, if there is anything I can still request of you, please try and heal him from his pain."

"Of course, Guidance; I would be more than willing to do that for you."

***

Night quickly closed in as Ember was led back to his cell. He had been careful to cooperate fully, not wanting to attract attention with the end so near, and now he stood alone in his little prison. Around him the other dragons were on the verge of dozing; many were lying on the floors of their cells and several were weeping quietly, as if trying to cry themselves to sleep. To his left, Ember saw that even Misery seemed tired and detached, as though her fire had burned down and left emptiness. Fearful lay curled up in the corner of his cage like usual.

Suddenly the doors at the far end of the building opened and Ember saw two men walking toward them, one of whom was Guidance.

"Fearful, my young friend; I have brought someone here to see you."

The dragon immediately picked up his head and looked at the man behind the trainer. *Justice, is that you?*

Guidance of course did not hear the question, but Justice did and he looked to Ember with surprise.

"Does he know me?"

I have spoken to him of you. He has been thinking long over my story, and just this evening asked me if he might be able to see you.

"Can you hear them?" asked Guidance, looking back and forth between them.

"Of course, I am the Dragon Rider. I have a Link just like Deception does," said Justice. He slowly turned to the blue dragon's cell and knelt down in front of it. "I heard that you wanted to speak with me?" he whispered kindly.

Slowly, the dragon got up and approached him. *Justice, Dragon Rider, I am honored to be able to talk with you. For a long time I have dwelt here, but for some reason I have never had any desire to leave. I had a harsh life, although others have suffered worse.*

"Tell me, what is your story?"

I was born to a small family that lived on a farm out in the county. For the first several years of my life I lived with them and as a hatchling played with the children. As I grew older, I helped their father plow his fields and do other work as well. I was stronger than all his horses put together—I was a great help to him. I lived with them for a long time; I watched the young kids I had played with grow up and become strong young adults, and with each turn of the seasons I was at their side. I was like a family pet or labor animal, but they loved me and I was happy there.

I think we all knew that the trappers would come eventually. Deception had come to power and was gathering all domesticated dragons to himself. The trappers offered to buy me from my family, but they did not wish to part with me and in the end they were all killed for their opposition. I watched it all, a blind panic overcoming me, and I wish to this day that I had fought to protect them. So many times I have longed to go back and change the moment, even if it would have cost me my life. But I did nothing; fear took hold of me and I was helpless.

Then the trappers tore me from the burnt wreckage of the farm and sold me to other people—soldiers in Deception's army—and they treated me badly. Day by day I was taught the cruelty of humans and by night I was left with my thoughts of despair and guilt, hating myself for my failure.

Deception led us on raids occasionally. I didn't think much of them; I didn't care. I was too lost in my own sorrow to see the destruction I caused. But then there was one attack I will never forget. It was to capture some city near the sea, and I was supposed to take men in to capture the gatehouse. When I landed, I behaved fiercely, attacking and killing all that came in range while my masters went about their business.

And then there was the man. He came for me without fear, without regard to life or limb. He ran to me even as I turned to destroy him, and he laid his hand on me—and then I felt love. It was the first time in so many years, and even in my younger days I had never experienced such a state of peace, of belonging, as I did in that moment.

Then the man was knocked away and my fear returned. I was led away from that place and never saw him again, but I always remembered that love, that it was possible someone might care for me again. After that I was brought back here where I have stayed, dwelling in my sorrow and my loss. But then Ember told me of his story, and I saw that even though he faced heartbreak and death he still clung to hope—hope that he could be loved again, even if only one last time. I want to do that now. I want to leave this place and see if someone might forgive me for what I've done, might keep me and call me as their own.

The weight of sorrow however is too deep for me to lift. But I was told that you have a way of purging Deception's influence; I hoped you might set me free.

Justice stared long into the dragon's eyes as he listened to his tale. At last he said softly, "That man who touched you was my brother; and as the Dragon Rider I am willing to help you—but do you know the cost?"

Yes, Ember explained it to me. But I would rather burn with agony under your wrath than live here under my sorrow.

Justice held his hand out. "Then try and look me in the eye."

The dragon nodded, breathed deeply, and pushed his snout against the outstretched hand. And fire coursed through him.

Ember watched from his cell as Fearful shrieked and whimpered, Justice bearing down on him. Some of the other dragons took notice, but Ember did not care. He watched with sympathy, knowing the pain, and was impressed with the dragon's determination. He seemed, despite his fear, even braver than he himself had been, and Ember couldn't help feeling guilty that he had waited so long to do the thing that the dragon before him had grasped so quickly as his only means of escape.

Slowly the pain seemed to die down and Fearful sank to the ground exhausted. Justice nodded and took away his hand. "For much of your life you have been ruled by fear," he said. "But now I set you free to live under men with joy."

He moved to the side and Guidance stepped forward, looking down upon his dragon with concern. "Fearful, are you all right?" he asked

The dragon got up slowly and his eyes widened, as though viewing the man with a new light. Guidance held his hand through the bars and Fearful immediately rubbed his head against it, a humming sound coming from deep within him.

Then suddenly the doors at the far end of the hall burst open with a loud bang and every dragons' head went up.

"Well, well, Dark Ranger!" shouted Deception as though he had just caught a criminal in the act. Around him stood a guard of seven soldiers, two with crossbows. "What a pleasant surprise to find you here! I was just about to send some of my men out to look for you, but that is no matter now. We can begin the process immediately. Come down here and we'll start at this end."

Justice, followed closely by Guidance, slowly turned away from Fearful and Ember as he began to make his way to the end of the hall. The soldiers quickly surrounded him as though he was about to be arrested. Deception smiled.

It was amazing how quickly the dragons seemed to wake up at the sight of the man. Instantly they each acted overcome with both sorrow and hunger at once, like a bunch of dogs begging for scraps of meat. Deception moved smoothly and quickly. One by one he laid his hand on every dragon and each time it would bow its head under him, drinking in his presence. Sometimes he would whisper things as well, and his words always seemed to have the effect of a snake charmer. One by one he moved down the line of dragons, and when he left, each one whined and moaned with more pain and heartbreak than before. But Deception never looked back.

Ember watched as he slowly made his way down the line until he came to Fearful's cage. The deep blue dragon looked at Deception differently than the others, almost as if he was a stranger. He came forward reluctantly and Ember noticed that Deception seemed confused at his behavior. He laid his hand on him in silence for several moments, but when he stopped, Fearful only snorted and moved to the back of his cage. Deception took a step back and eyed him with confusion.

"Guidance, there is something wrong with that one," he said sharply. "He was hiding his thoughts from me. I want you to look into that at once!"

"Of course, sire," said Guidance quickly with a small bow.

They came to Ember's cage, and the dragon suddenly realized that his heart was beating very quickly. He tried to shield his thoughts, knowing Deception wore his Link, and looked into his eyes as though he were some dumb, frightened beast.

"Is this one new?" asked Deception, staring at Ember closely.

"Yes, I would say he came in, oh, sometime within the last week or so," said Guidance.

Deception stared into the dragon's eyes even harder. Ember felt fear coursing through him now. He wanted to look at Justice, but he didn't dare, afraid of letting Deception know his thoughts.

"You look strangely familiar," he said. His eyes narrowed. "I wonder if..." He turned to Guidance. "Is there anything in particular you think I might like to know about this dragon? About his wing perhaps?"

Ember instinctively folded his wings tighter against his sides. The air seemed very still.

"Why yes, I took him out for flying only this evening," said Guidance in a rather careless manner. "He flew wondrously; you should have seen him."

"Really..." said Deception slowly, his eyes still locked on Ember's wing.

"Well, if you'd like, I can bring him out and show him to you."

There was a pause of several seconds.

"No, that's not necessary," said Deception at length. "It doesn't matter. All will soon be revealed." He held out his hand through the bars.

Ember swallowed and moved forward. This was it. Secretly he was glad that Guidance had gotten the time to polish his scales with oil so that they glimmered in the light in a more natural manner. But he must not allow himself to think about that. He was afraid. Yes! Concentrate on that! It would be normal for any dragon to be nervous if this was its first time with Deception. Hold on; try to act natural...

He moved forward and allowed Deception to touch his muzzle.

Of course, the feelings came instantly. Ember tried to cut through them, but oh how pleasant they were! Feelings of joy, of elation, of hunger—*No! I have something better than hunger now.* The feelings continued to pour down on him. His heart beat wildly. He thought briefly of Justice, but suddenly he didn't seem to matter anymore. No one did. All that mattered was joy and desire. What else did he need? What else could he want? *No! This isn't about what I want.* It wasn't about him. This was about others, and the promises he had made them. He would die for something greater than pleasure.

Yes. He would die! *Pain; drown the pleasure in pain!* Ember tried to hold the thought in his head. He was about to die, he had only a few more days to live, and his final trip tomorrow would seal his fate.

A mistake! The flow of pleasure and elation immediately melded into comfort and consolation. *Sorrow! I've awakened sorrow!* He tried to counter it, but felt no desire to. He felt peace and rest. He wouldn't have to die. He was safe here. Deception would protect him; he need never return to the King. What was he thinking by going with Justice the final step? It wasn't too late yet! He could still live—live a full life! Just reveal Justice now and the nightmare would be over. He would be free!

Up until this point Ember's thoughts had been hurried and tangled, impossible for anyone to read even with a Link. But now he began to slow down and his mind became clearer. He would tell Deception. Everything would be all right. His heart felt suddenly calm, his body suddenly still. He turned a final glance to Justice, the man he was about to destroy, whose hand burned like fire. The man who was his Rider.

Ember stopped. His Rider. He could throw him off now, he could have him killed, he could be free of ownership. But in the furthest depth of his heart, Ember knew that ownership was only there because he had chosen it, because for some impossible reason he had once been willing to trade his life in order to be under the rule of that man, if only for a while. If he had chosen it once, there must have been a reason—one that perhaps the pleasure made it too difficult to remember. Ember closed his eyes and bowed his head. *What I have chosen, I have chosen. I will not turn from that path now.*

Whether this single isolated phrase meant anything to Deception or not, it was the only thing he heard from the dragon. The rest of the time Ember was silent, a peaceful surrender calming his mind. The two of them stayed like that for several minutes, but nothing changed. Slowly, Deception withdrew his hand and Ember opened his eyes.

"I...I—" Deception began, greatly confused. "I don't understand. I was certain that—I thought..." he stared at Ember for several more moments, but then turned in a resigned sort of way to the next cage.

"What's the matter?" asked Justice. "Were you looking for something?"

"I was, but...I guess I was wrong."

The party moved down to the next cage and Ember allowed himself to sink to the ground. He had done it. Barely, but he had resisted. He turned his eyes to Justice and felt a stab of guilt. Had he really been so close to betraying the man who had risked so much for him? He shivered with the idea.

To his left he was vaguely aware of Misery being processed, and he turned to see her facing Deception and humming quietly, his hand on her head. Suddenly a wave of panic washed over Ember. She knew! She was one of only two dragons he had told his story to and she knew! What was she telling Deception right now? What wouldn't she tell to gain his support, his favor? Anxiously he watched the two of them in silence, his heart beating wildly. Then Deception turned away and moved to the next cage in line, appearing almost as disappointed as before.

Misery turned to look at him. "Just this once," she whispered. "I let you off this one time; but if I hear anything more about your Rider, or his kingdom, you can be sure that Deception will be the first to know."

"Thank you," said Ember, bowing his head slightly. "I am indebted to you."

"I don't want your indebtedness," she snapped. "I want no part in any of this. If you want to go along with that man so that he kills you, then that is none of my concern." She turned away and lay down, facing forward through her bars at the opposite wall.

Deception continued down the line of dragons, but he never found what he was looking for. When he got to the end, he seemed lost and confused.

"Shall we move on to the other prison houses?" asked Justice politely. "Or is that all that you wanted me for?"

"No, let's keep going. It might be that perhaps...then again, maybe I was wrong."

Slowly, Deception began to make his way to the doors of the building. His footsteps fell heavily like those of a defeated man, and his head was bowed slightly. As he was reaching to open the door however, he stopped suddenly and looked at his hand. He rubbed his fingers together.

"Guidance," he said, turning, "have you been putting oil on these dragons?"

The Dragon Trainer seemed to flounder for just a second at the question, but then he composed himself. "Well, yes sire. Some of the dragons do not have scales that shine as brightly as others; given that they will be ridden into battle tomorrow, I wanted to make sure they all looked presentable."

"Indeed," said Deception slowly, gazing thoughtfully at his hand. He looked back up at Ember. "Some scales do not shine as brightly…"

He suddenly turned to one of the soldiers. "I want that dragon moved to the forward hold. Ensure that he will be counted among those attacking in the second wave."

"Yes, my lord," said the solider with a bow. He and another man broke off from the group and began to unlock the dragon's cage. Deception turned and marched out into the night with his party close behind them; the doors closed with a dull echo.

***

Later that night, as midnight neared and the sky grew darker, two figures met in the cover of an alley. They were Justice and Guidance.

"I can't believe we made it through that," said Guidance with relief.

"It was all thanks to your tricks," said Justice. "Only a Dragon Trainer would have thought of the things you did."

"I fear my tricks may have done more harm than good," said Guidance. "He noticed the oil."

"Yes, but I still don't think he knows. He is just suspicious enough to want Ember where he can watch him. You did well, and I think I will be able to handle the battle tomorrow."

"That is good, I am glad that I was able to help you and Highland."
There was silence for several moments.

"What is the matter?" asked Justice finally. "You seem sad."

"It's just..." said Guidance. "It's just that I was thinking about Fearful. What will become of him tomorrow? Deception will have all of the dragons in the attack, and he will be killed—along with every other beast that I have cared for all these years."

"You wish to save him?"

"Yes. But not only he; there are others also—dragons that I have known since they were small, that I longed so often to see free of this place and their sadness. I think that I love Fearful most of all, but there are others that I cannot bear to leave, that I cannot bear to abandon to their death."

"Then save them," said Justice after a pause. "Save them before they are drafted into battle tomorrow."

"But how? I cannot take any dragons out by myself, and it is too late

now. None of the guards would let me through the gates at this time of night with one, much less many, dragons."

"Perhaps you could encourage them to do so."

"How?"

"With this." Justice held up a large bag of gold.

Guidance stared at it with wide eyes. "How ever did you get that?"

"Oh, Ember helped. The important thing however is that I will have no need for it where I am going. Divide it among the guards, and I'll come along just in case they try to double-cross you."

"Oh, thank you, Justice! I am more indebted to you than I can possibly ever repay."

"Think nothing of it. Do you know which ones you'll save and where they are? We won't be able to take many."

"Yes, I know. Many dragons would not want to leave anyway, but I think I know which ones will trust me."

"Good. I will go around with you and see if I can reclaim any of their hearts from Deception's influence tonight, and then I will help you to escape with them. After that, hide until the battle is over tomorrow and then come and surrender yourselves to Highland's force. I will see to it that you escape the wrath of the King."

"Thank you, Justice; I will begin making preparations immediately."

"Yes, go; I will join you shortly. There's one thing that I need to do first."

* * *

Ember lay in his cell in the darkened building. The cage was similar to his last in size, but it was not situated near any other dragons. He could still hear them through the blackness, some moving and others sleeping, but he seemed to be in a corner by himself. He felt lonely in that place, so he spoke through the Link telling of what it was like and how he felt. He had nearly lulled himself to sleep with his thoughts when some instinct made him sit up and strain to see through the darkness.

Justice? Is that you?

"Yes, it is I," came his voice. He moved closer, and by the light of a single moonbeam cast through a barred window Ember saw his face.

I was afraid that you would not come.

"Of course I'd come, especially since this is your last night here."

Ember nodded and moved forward toward his prison door. Justice reached through the bars and stroked the dragon's muzzle gently.

Did Deception figure out who I am?

"No, I think he is only suspicious. But that was through our mistake, not yours. Tomorrow you will be led to the battle lines, and I will meet you there. Together we will fly out one last time as Rider and dragon."

Yes, we will; once more...

"I'm sorry, Ember," said Justice sadly. "I tried, I really tried—but I cannot go against the law. I want to save you; I would if it were possible, but I...I cannot." His voice choked.

I understand, and I do not hold it against you. It was through no fault of yours that this has come upon me.

"Then you will fly with me? You no longer fear death?"

I think I will always fear death, just like any animal. But if I am to die, then there is no other place I would rather do so than at your side and by your hand. You are my Rider, and I desire to be with you more than I desire to prolong my life.

"Then you are very brave, my Ember. I will ensure that when tales are told of you, they will remember your courage. You will die a Rider's dragon."

Ember nodded and looked down. Slowly, a great tear fell from his eye and splashed gently on the ground.

"What's the matter, my dear friend?"

I was just thinking...the two of us would have made a great pair.

"Aye, we would have," said Justice softly, resting his cheek against his dragon's snout. A tear fell from his eye as well. "One of the greatest."

Then may we ride triumphantly tomorrow.

"Yes. One more time."

Ember looked deep into his master's eyes.

My Eldar.

"My Eldar."

7

Dragon Rider

The building was full of noise and the shouts of men when Ember awoke. He opened his eyes to see soldiers moving here and there, yelling orders to each other and unlocking cages. He rose to his feet nervously as he watched, careful to mask his expression. This was it; today was the day he and Justice had been journeying toward; today would mark their last flight together.

Ember followed the men obediently when they unlocked his cage. In his heart he could still feel the worry, the apprehension for the battle ahead, but despite it all he was determined not to show fear. Whatever was to come, his decision was finally made. He was Justice's dragon, and nothing could shake that now.

A moment later Ember was led outside and made to stand in a line along with the other dragons. He made no attempt to communicate with any of them; instead he stared out ahead and watched as the men went about their confused attempts to organize the beasts and assign them all riders.

It would have been a lot easier if Guidance had been there, but he was missing—along with several of the other dragons he had been closest to. No one seemed to know what had happened, and Ember watched with amusement as they tried to control the beasts without him. They certainly obeyed the men without much fuss, but many of the dragons weren't as calm without their trainer. That, and there was a feeling of nervousness in the air. All knew that they were going to war, that it was a battle they were being organized for, and every man and dragon seemed to be restless with the electricity of it. Ember was no exception, and he tried not to shift uneasily as he waited.

Soon all the dragons were in a line, and Ember was led with them toward the city gates that opened to the northern battlefield. Several times their march stopped for some unseen holdup. No one fully knew what was going on, so Ember continued to follow, obeying orders and moving along as he was told. But secretly he began to contact Justice, telling him his thoughts and where he was.

During one of their stops toward the gates, each dragon was assigned a rider that came and stood by their side. Ember was given a short stout man he had never seen before who spoke gruffly and briefly when at all. Together they moved on as the line did, not even bothering to look at one another. Ember was a bit surprised that Justice had not somehow managed to work his way into the group so they would be assigned together. Come to think of it, he had not seen Justice at all so far. Where could he be?

Still however Ember trusted that he would show up, that when the time came, they would ride together. He kept up his silent communication, telling his Rider everything he saw and heard.

Ember began to wonder if any of the other dragons knew their rider, if any of them had practiced with the one who would soon lead them into battle. It seemed so strange, so odd to him that the dragons would be ridden by someone whom they had not fought with before, whom they had not grown up with, whom they did not love. How was such an arrangement even supposed to work? Did the riders just expect their mounts to obey their commands like some winged horse? Were the dragons trained to follow their leaders mindlessly? None of the dragons even appeared to care about the battle, the riders, or their lives. They were so wrapped up in their own inward thoughts and sorrows that they allowed themselves to be led like stupid beasts.

At one point, Deception walked down the line, talking to some generals as he went. Ember quickly lowered his head and tried not to make eye contact. He had come too far to have things ruined now. But Deception passed by without even noticing him, and Ember looked back up in relief. The man wasn't looking for him—he was too caught up in the battle, in his final war. For so long he had planned this moment that he no longer seemed to care about one little dragon he had lost. What mattered to him now, no doubt, was just mustering his forces to face the King.

Soon the line began to travel through the gates and Ember's eyes were dazzled by the expanse of the battlefield. For mile upon mile there was nothing but the smooth, flat field of grass that seemed to spread out in every direction without end. Directly ahead of him he saw the dragons moving into formation and beyond them the countless ranks of Deception's army. No doubt he had summoned together the soldiers from every kingdom in the Shadowlands to form the greatest opposing force ever to be recorded in history. Ember waited as he was ushered into formation behind the first line of dragons, and then strained to see past them to the forces of Highland.

They were an amazing sight to behold! Far ahead on the other end of the field stood Glory with the King upon her back. They did not charge or fly but stood alone at the head of the army. There were no other dragons to see on their side, but the force of soldiers gathered under the King's command told Ember that he must have brought not only

Highland's army, but those of many of the other kingdoms as well, those that still chose to ally with him.

But as he looked, Ember couldn't help but feel a slight pang of hopelessness. How did the King hope to stand against so many? Perhaps he was equal in the way of men, but Deception had over fifty dragons under his command and still the King stood alone with only Glory by his side. What would become of him?

From somewhere there was a shout and each of the riders mounted their dragon. Ember felt his man pulling himself up onto his back and tried to hide his disgust. He looked behind himself and saw several more ranks of dragons, each armed with a rider and ready to set out. Ember looked forward again. Soon they would be given the call to attack.

Justice, where are you?

***

Deception made his way to the front of his forces, riding a dragon. Out of all of them he had chosen one that was black like midnight, similar to Glory. Of course, his beast was less than half her size, but it had seemed like the best choice. Ideally he would have preferred to ride Ember, but the confounded dragon had escaped him and was still missing. Well, maybe.

Deception turned to look at the blue dragon in the second rank, the one that had been mysteriously covered in oil the previous night. Aye, there was even some of it on him now, intermixed with patches that did not seem to shine as if there was something wrong with his scales. Deception looked at him curiously, squinting almost as if that would allow him to see right through the beast. He did seem so familiar...but it couldn't be Ember, could it? A dragon's scales did not simply change color, and of course Ember would be unable to fly. Only Guidance had the skills to fix a dragon's wing, and he wouldn't turn against him, would he? Deception frowned. Then again, the Dragon Trainer had mysteriously disappeared...

Deception looked forward again. No, Justice was not here. That dragon had one of his own riders, and Ember would not be willing to fly under any other command. Deception looked out ahead at the King's forces. He would win. There was no doubt about it. If the King fell, his men would retreat and all would be over.

But Deception couldn't quell the unease growing in his stomach. He looked about at his forces of dragons, surely impossible to overcome, but still he remained worried. He didn't know why; maybe it was that this was it, that he had finally arrived at the end of his plan. Kill the King, and Highland was his!

Slowly, Deception drew forth his saber and held it high. The front line of dragons, his ten strongest, tensed at the ready. He could do this! The King would die! Highland would fall!

Deception grunted and brought his sword down. The ten dragons immediately leaped into the air, their riders spurring them on. Time to show the King what he was made of!

***

Ember watched intently as the front line of dragons took off. Soon he would be next, and then it would be impossible for Justice to get to him. He shifted nervously in place. He wasn't sure why Deception did not have all his dragons fly off at once; perhaps he felt confident that ten would be enough to overcome the King—and perhaps he was right. Across the field, Ember saw Glory slowly rising into the air, her great wings flapping majestically and powerfully. Ember continued to watch, spellbound, waiting to see what would happen when the oncoming assault reached her.

"I'm afraid that you will need to dismount," came a voice.

"What are you doing here, Dark Ranger?" Ember heard his rider ask.

Ember smiled and turned his head to see Justice alongside him, still disguised in his black cloak.

"I said that you will need to come down," the Dark Ranger said. "You have been reassigned."

"Reassigned?" cried the man in rage. "On whose authority?"

The Dark Ranger's eyes narrowed. "My own."

"Why you—! You think you can just come here and...and..." He slid down Ember's back, quivering in rage. The Dark Ranger reached within the folds of his cloak as the man drew his sword.

"Away with you!" the short man cried, swinging his weapon hard at the figure, which ducked, leaped nimbly around, and whacked him on the head with the hilt of a katana. The man fell to the ground with a thump. The black figure then smoothly sheathed his sword and pulled himself up onto the dragon's back as though nothing had happened. Ember quickly stepped to the side so that he stood over the fallen body.

What a relief to see you, Justice.

"It's nice to see you too," he whispered. Ember heard him tinkering with something and a minute later felt the Link around his neck.

Won't someone see this? he asked apprehensively.

No; everyone's too busy watching the fight, and even if they did it's too late to do anything.

Ember nodded and looked up at the sky above the battlefield. The ten dragons had just about reached Glory who hovered in the air waiting for them. They were each half her size; of course they were smaller—they had all hatched shortly after Deception had arrived in the Shadowlands, which was already well after Glory's birth.

Will the King be all right? asked Ember.

Of course he will; don't worry. I doubted him once, and I'll never do it again.

The dragons collided and fire seemed to explode, though all was too far away to hear. Ember was surprised to see first one, and then another

of the dragons fall fluttering from the sky. Through the smoke, he could see the others floundering around the great black dragon, unable to get closer as she fended them off with great blasts of air from her powerful wings.

The King is up there too, said Justice. *He's leaping from one dragon to another and slaying their riders. The dragons have great strength, but they are without guidance or direction. They fight because they are forced to, and they do not have the determination that the King's dragon does. She will be able to overpower them.*

Suddenly there was the sound of a horn and Ember saw the dragons around him tense. He crouched with them, preparing to leap with the second wave of the assault. Up above, Ember saw the remaining dragons break off their attack and begin to retreat. He saw Deception raise his sword.

When he gives the signal, Justice said, *move with the rest of the charge. We'll try to escape once in the air.*

Ember nodded and along with every other dragon and rider watched Deception. Everyone seemed to hold their breath.

The sword came down.

Instantly Ember was in the air along with the other dragons. They rose up together, their formation breaking down into a confusing mass of scaly bodies and flapping wings. Ember knew that anyone would be able to see the scar on his left wing now, but he did not care. No one was watching them anyway.

Fly above the others, he heard Justice say.

Obediently he began to angle his path so that he rose higher. Up ahead he saw the King upon Glory, hovering patiently in the distance as behind them there suddenly rose a great cloud of griffins who had been positioned behind the soldiers. Ember looked down briefly and saw, between the dragons, Deception's army on the move, charging forward to meet the forces of Highland.

Ember looked forward again and continued to fly higher. He was almost above the others and was slowly beginning to pull back as well, letting the rest of the dragons move ahead. He briefly caught a glimpse of one in the mass who looked like Misery, and a pang came to his heart. But she had made it clear that she wanted no part with him, so he let her go.

You're doing well! Keep moving higher and farther back. Let the others go on ahead; they won't notice us.

Ember obeyed and soon they were completely above the charge, watching the horde of flying beasts head for the King.

Good! Now veer off to the left and go around. I want to avoid the conflicts between them and my father.

Why couldn't we stay and fight? asked Ember. *We could help him.*

He doesn't need help, and I'm more concerned about keeping you safe than I am about him. I know you wish to redeem your legacy, but right now the best way of doing that is to listen to me and to land behind Highland's forces.

Of course, said Ember understandingly, and began to pull to the left, breaking off completely from the main charge.

Keep flying higher too, said Justice. *They won't see us if we are above them, but it will still help to keep a safe distance from all of this.*

Ember nodded and continued to fly higher, panting in the thinning air. Both dragon and Rider were focused on their escape. Neither thought to look behind them.

***

Deception flew swiftly through the air, spurring his dragon to catch up with the one that had broken away. He was fairly sure now that there was a scar on that dragon's left wing. And the rider looked different too. He could be the one! Deception allowed himself to smile and continued to urge his dragon on. Yes, his target was smaller and lighter, but if that was Ember, he would be too out of practice to fly at full speed. He could be overtaken!

Deception stole a fleeting glance to the side and saw what he most feared. His dragons were in disarray. They pounded at the King from all sides, but none were able to reach him, none were able to overcome Glory. Many had already lost their riders and were flying about in confusion, screeching at nothing in particular and venting their fire into the open air. Those that tried to retreat were set upon by scores of griffins, all striking with precise attacks around their King.

Deception growled. So, his plan would fail. Just as in the deepest depths of his heart he feared it would, knew it would. But it mattered not; he always had a backup plan. For a while he'd given up hope of it, felt that the direct attack would be his only way, but now if he really had found Ember...

He needed to be sure. Yes, the dragon seemed just like Ember, he was about the right size and there was the scarred wing, but he had to remove all doubt. Deception's eyes narrowed. Justice might have disguised his color using the die from the bleeding plant, which would have turned green scales blue. But there was only one way to know for sure. Deception spurred his dragon higher, even higher than before. They didn't notice him. They wouldn't notice him. Not until it was too late. Deception smiled and gave the command.

His dragon dove.

***

Justice felt it through his Link. Before he had been too focused on moving ahead, on getting Ember to safety. But suddenly he felt the thoughts of a second dragon, one intent on blasting them with fire.

Ember! Look out!

Suddenly flames rained down upon them. Justice instinctively ducked under the hood of his cloak and Ember folded his wings protectively and dove as fire poured down along the extent of his body. A moment later, a black dragon shot over their heads, leveling out and preparing to turn around. Justice quickly threw off his blazing cloak, letting it flutter away in the wind, and looked around at his dragon in horror.

Ember had snapped his wings back open, breaking their dive, but now his scales were ablaze, the oil on them ignited in flame. Justice felt his dragon shudder in the searing pain as he tried to angle himself upward again. He seemed able to bear the heat along his back and legs, but as the fire died down and began to disappear, Justice saw that the dye had been burned away, leaving the scales a vivid, if not slightly blackened, green.

***

Deception laughed wildly as his dragon turned around. Yes! There was no doubt now! Ember was here, right under his nose! Quickly he altered the course of his mount so they would fly over the other dragon.

He drew his saber. Yes! This was it! He tensed, waiting for just the right moment as Ember approached below.

And then he jumped.

***

Justice saw him coming and quickly drew his katana, taking a shaky stance atop his flying mount. Then Deception landed, his feet hitting Ember's lower back between his wings.

Justice growled at him, but Deception said nothing, choosing rather to crouch down and grip one of Ember's spikes with his free hand.

Justice had barely enough time to eye him curiously before he heard Ember cry out and a moment later found himself hanging on for dear life as the black dragon collided with them.

***

Ember had been distracted by the man landing on his back, and so had not reacted quickly enough when Deception's mount dove for him. Now they were interlocked, claws gripping each other's shoulders, teeth biting at each other's necks. Fire blasted in both directions and panic sized Ember's mind as the larger dragon overpowered him.

Help me! I can't do this!

Yes, you can Ember; fight him off!

He's got me by the neck, there's nothing I can do!

I didn't bring you all this way just to have you fall five miles from safety! Do something!

I can't, he's too strong; he's got me in a hold!

Oh Ember, Ember, came a new voice, a feminine one—one that he had not heard for nearly three years. *Have you forgotten so quickly everything I taught you?*

Ember tried to calm himself, tried to slow his breathing even with the beast's jaws locked around his neck. He carefully looked around and spotted one of the dragon's beating wings. With careful aim, he blasted it with fire.

The other beast screeched in agony, letting go of Ember's neck as its wing was torn to shreds by the flame. Quickly Ember folded his own wings, preventing a counterattack, and the two of them dropped from the skies, still fighting and clutching each other in their claws.

The black dragon blasted Ember again and again in the face, but he didn't return the attack, instead choosing to angle downward as their dive grew steeper, their speed grew faster, the ground drew nearer. The other dragon continued to claw at Ember's unprotected neck and belly, but still he held on, watching the grass below approach them with un-fathomable speed.

And then in one instant, Ember delivered a savage kick to his opponent's chest and snapped his own wings open, breaking the dive. The sudden jolt tore the black dragon off and left him falling at much the same speed as before, madly flapping his useless wing as he hurled toward the battlefield.

Ember screeched in pain as he forced his wings straight. The stitches barely held as he managing to level out just above the grass. Frantically, he tried to sense if Justice had managed to hold on as he angled back upward again.

Justice! Are you there?

Yes, I'm fine. Good job—I knew you could do it!

Is Deception still there?

Yes, he is. Don't worry about him; just head back up. Try to reach the same height as before!

I will. Are you sure you will be all right? Do you need my help?

No; I will take care of him! Just concentrate on flying!

Ember nodded and continued to head for the skies.

***

Justice stood carefully, straddling his dragon's spikes as he faced his enemy. Across from him Deception stood with easy balance between Ember's beating wings. He twirled his sword absentmindedly.

"You ought to congratulate yourself, Justice," he said smiling. "You've made it so far. Even to sneak out on the very day of my attack."

"Look around you!" growled Justice. "You failed! Can't you see that you are defeated?"

Deception looked at him sadly. "Yes, I know. It appears that all this time, in all my lies and tricks, the one I had really been deceiving was myself." He looked out toward the King, and Justice followed his gaze.

The assault had fallen to pieces. The dragons were scattered and wild with fear and confusion. Griffins descended upon those that broke away and tore apart their wings. Several of the beasts still dove for Glory, but none seemed able to reach her. The great blasts of air from her wings kept them out of range, and there was always the King, leaping from one to another and dealing death with every strike of his great sword.

"I was so sure..." said Deception, "I was so sure I could do it, that somehow if I gathered enough force, I could overcome the King. All a vain fantasy."

"Then you admit you have lost!" said Justice coldly, turning back to him. "You see that all of your efforts have been futile!"

"Not so!" barked Deception. He advanced forward a step, holding his saber at the ready. "For you see, I have found Ember again, the last connection to the Dragon Rider. The Pact hangs by a thread; if he is killed before you can be named his Rider, then the tradition Highland has used for over two thousand years will be broken. You may take for yourself a new dragon, but the original will be gone, the link to the past destroyed!"

"I will not let you have him," growled Justice, his voice low and threatening.

Deception laughed as he advanced another step.

"All right, Dragon Rider, I will tell you how this will go. First, I will slay you and cast you down from my dragon. Then I will bring him back under my control with a touch of my hand and all your work will be lost!

And finally, with you gone and Ember at my command, I will fly us both in a direct assault against the King. In one fatal moment, your father will have to choose whether to die, or to destroy in one blast both me and Ember, dissolving the Pact forever! I may die, but I will die in victory!"

"Not on my watch you won't!" cried Justice, and with a quick lunge he struck out against Deception, who blocked him—and their greatest battle began.

Justice was the better swordsman, but he was also unfortunately the more inexperienced at fighting atop a flying dragon. Deception had practiced much in the past and was able to easily keep his footing on the slippery scales as he leapt nimbly about. Justice was forced to rely on his speed more than ever before to block, to duck, and to counter strikes. The two of them were a very close match in the sky, and neither seemed to gain the upper hand.

Justice battled fiercely, employing every trick, every skill he knew, and sweat dripped down his face as he was blocked again and again by an opponent equally as desperate, equally as strained.

And then it happened. Justice had only a second to react when he felt the impulse through the Link.

"No Ember! No!" he cried as his dragon suddenly dove with a reckless spin. With a desperate lunge, Justice barely managed to catch hold of one of Ember's spikes, the twist nearly throwing him out into empty space. His katana was torn from his hand and disappeared into the spinning vortex of wind.

Ember! Stop! This isn't helping! he cried.

With a shudder Ember broke his dive and leveled out again. Justice quickly pulled himself to his feet and saw Deception shakily doing the same. Both of them had barely managed to react in time to the dragon's impulse, but Deception had expected Ember to do something of the sort while Justice had not—which was why Deception had managed to keep a grip on his saber.

Ember! What do you think you were doing?

I was trying to throw him off! It seemed like you needed help.

Help? You've made things worse!

Deception laughed as he slowly approached, his saber extended. "It looks like the two of you still haven't figured out how to work together," he said.

Justice growled and drew his dagger.

I'm sorry, came Ember's voice. *I didn't mean to—*

Just fly straight! shouted Justice angrily. *Let me handle this; don't try any more tricks!*

Deception laughed wildly as he brought his saber down on the dagger. Justice swept it away and launched a counterstrike. But now he was at a disadvantage. His lost weapon gave his assailant the chance he needed to drive him back.

Desperately Justice blocked swing after swing, until suddenly he found his foot slipping on the curve of Ember's back and the dizzying drop of open space behind his head. He tried to surge forward, but Deception took his chance and brought his saber down on the flat of Justice's dagger. With both hands, Justice strained back against the weight, his balance teetering. He felt Ember try to tilt slightly in flight so that his footing would be less steep.

Deception grinned as he bore down on him. "Ah, this looks familiar," he said mockingly. "Let me think—Oh! I remember! This is what your brother did to me just before he threw me down, casting me away from my dragon. Seems like such an irony now, doesn't it?" He smiled down at Justice who grunted desperately to push back the saber, to keep his balance.

Deception grinned. "You're defeated, Justice." He leaded in close and whispered, his voice filled with hate: "...And I cast you out!"

Then with a final push, Justice was flung headlong into the air, his dagger spinning away from him, and his expression one of horror.

Justice! No! cried Ember, as he folded his wings and plummeted into a mad dive after his Rider.

Deception was thrown back as he caught hold of one of the spikes, laughing wildly. "Come on Ember!" he roared as he held on. "Don't you remember me?" He pulled himself up with a jerk and raised his weapon high, "Or maybe you're too distracted."

He brought his saber down on the chain around Ember's neck and the severed Link fell away in the wind. "Let's see how well you do without him!" he cried and placed his hand flat on Ember's scales.

Justice watched as he fell, as his dragon dove down after him, closing the distance. He saw Deception clinging to his back.

Ember! he called. *Resist him!*

But the dragon did not seem to hear. He still dove after his Rider, his eyes determined, but Justice could feel the war raging in his head, the feelings of pleasure, of hunger, of a sad longing.

"No Ember!" he cried. "Fight him off!" but his words were lost in the wind.

The dragon had nearly reached him, his claws extended to grab him. But then his eyes seemed to change. They flickered, jumping from determined to passive, then back.

"No...come on..." Justice reached out to touch his beast, his hand only a few inches from its scales.

And then he felt Ember's voice, burdened and pressed down by the weight of the emotions: *I'm sorry—I'm so sorry Justice...*

And then he seemed to give up altogether and the dragon's eyes turned from passive to cruel.

Justice stared at them in shock. "No!"

Then the dragon snapped open its great wings and shot away into the distant heights above.

***

From his mount, the King watched as the dragon swooped away, as the tiny figure continued to fall. The assault had ended, the dragons had been scattered, his griffins had flown off after the survivors. Now he watched alone as his eldest son fell to his doom, as the dragon Peace had died saving flew off under Deception's control.

Which shall we save? he felt Glory ask. *We can only reach one in time.*

The King stared out at the two, growing farther apart by the second. Then with a heavy heart he spoke to his dragon: *Ember was given his chance. I lost one son already in saving him—shall I lose my other as well?*

Glory nodded and made a dive for the falling figure.

* * *

Deception righted himself at the crook of Ember's neck. The dragon shuddered and trembled beneath him, but he was under his control. Deception allowed himself to smile as he slowly steered his mount back around in a circle. There was the King, just about to reach his falling son. Soon they would be back up again and both would watch as he made his final attack.

He tried to guide Ember in their direction, and the dragon reacted hesitantly. He wasn't adjusting quite like he used to. Deception wished that he still had the Curse, but it didn't matter. All he needed now was for Ember to make one last charge toward Glory and it would all be over. The King himself would destroy the Dragon Rider Pact! Deception grinned as he continued to guide his mount in a collision course with the great black dragon. Yes! Ember seemed to be responding better now! They would do it! Together—one last time!

* * *

Justice rode alongside the King, watching as the green dragon in the distance grew closer. Glory was flying in a straight course toward him now, and in a few minutes they would collide.

"He is going to try and ram into us," said the King. "If he manages to stab Glory through the heart, we will all be killed."

"Then break off!" shouted Justice over the wind. "Avoid a collision!"

"I can't," said the King. "Glory is more powerful, but Ember is smaller and faster. If we do not engage directly, Ember will outmaneuver us."

"But you'll kill him!"

"I know, but I cannot have Glory killed and all of Highland thrown into turmoil. Deception must be stopped, even if it means killing Ember too."

"But that's what he wants!" cried Justice in desperation. "Deception wants you to kill them both! It's part of his plan! The Dragon Rider Pact will be destroyed!"

"It can be rebuilt; it has to be. There is no other choice."

"Please!" begged Justice. "There has to be some other way."

"There is none."

Up ahead, the dragon continued to approach at a reckless speed.

***

Ember was not completely taken. Down in the furthest depths of his mind, where there was neither light nor perception, a fragmented part of his consciousness still fought against Deception's influence. Ember didn't know why he fought; most of him had already given in. Yet still he struggled blindly in the dark. He had the vague impression that he was flying, that he was moving quickly, but he couldn't tell. He didn't know where he was or what was happening. All he knew was that trembling pleasure suffocated him, surrounded him, embraced him. Everywhere he could feel the hunger, the burning desire that filled him with life and energy. The longing for...for...he couldn't tell, he didn't know. He didn't know anything. Nothing except that for some reason he had to fight it.

Ember struggled against the pressure. He didn't want to resist; he wanted, more than anything, to give in. Yet part of him would not be put to rest. He couldn't reason, he couldn't see, he couldn't think. He needed help, understanding. Somewhere, in the very back of his mind, he seemed to recall a Rider. What happened to him? He could not remember. Maybe he was out there somewhere. Maybe he could help.

With all his might, Ember struggled to form a single word.

Justice...

***

Deception was too preoccupied in his attack to notice what Ember was thinking. Up ahead was the King. Soon they would collide. Deception would raise his hands, feel himself and Ember enveloped in fire, and die knowing he had won! For a second, Deception wondered if the King wouldn't attack, if he would be so taken off guard that he wouldn't react in time. Maybe Ember would actually make it to Glory! Perhaps the King really would be killed!

Deception smiled and shook his head. No, it wasn't possible. The King would kill them. But what did it matter? He was victorious either way. He had won!

***

"Ember!" cried Justice. "I heard him! He's trying to fight Deception off! Can't you hear him?"

"I do, but it makes no difference."

"How can you say that? Peace died to save him! I swore that I would try and lead him home! Don't make me go back on my oath!"

"You're not going back on your oath," said the King curtly. "You promised to try and lead him back, and try you have. Now he has chosen once again to return to his old master, and he will pay the price."

"Please," begged Justice. "I wanted so badly to save him. Can't you give him another chance?"

"I have already given him many chances. Ember committed treason. You've known from the beginning that his life is forfeit, even if reclaimed; what difference does it make if he dies now?"

"There was no trial! It's not fair!"

"There is no trial to conduct. Ember's guilt is clear; there is no one to advocate for him."

"You can't know that!"

"Of course I do!"

"I would find him a defendant!" yelled Justice. "I'll find somebody."

"There is no one that would do it. Who would stand for that condemned dragon? Who would dare to fight a case where there was no hope? There is no one to advocate for him."

"Then I will!" cried Justice. "I will advocate for him."

The King stared at him coldly. Ember was just moments away.

"You would abandon your own sense of justice? For years you have upheld the law—you would throw that away? For him? Why?"

"Because I love him," said Justice, staring out at the oncoming dragon, the outline of Deception now clear upon his back. "Because I would give anything to see that he had one more chance."

The King placed a hand on his shoulder.

"My son, today you have become worthy of the crown."

With a sudden jerk, Glory swooped upward.

***

Deception couldn't believe it. Glory was pulling up! The King wasn't going to kill them. He had just surrendered his life! With a cry he pulled Ember up to follow and ducked as the dragon's horns cut two long gashes along Glory's belly.

***

Justice dropped to his knees to keep his balance as Glory shuddered, bellowing in pain as she tried to keep from dropping. Behind them, the form of Ember shot out and began a dive to double back.

Through his Link, Justice heard the words of his dragon: *Justice—I'm...I'm sorry—I can't resist...*

***

In the darkness of his mind, Ember thought for a moment he felt his horns drag against something, but it meant nothing to him. Desperately he struggled to communicate with his Rider. *Justice—I'm...I'm sorry—I can't resist...*

He thought he could feel himself in a dive, but he wasn't sure. The pleasure was intoxicating, it felt like a lullaby. *There was a time where I would have been content to live with these feelings forever...*

But why not now? What had changed? Ember struggled to remember. Why should he care for others? If he had pleasure what did it matter? He could forget everything else and live in happiness if he'd just let it all go.

***

Deception had forced Ember into a dive and now pulled him up again. Above was the great black dragon. They had her now! Deception let out a cry and spurred Ember upward faster and faster, aiming for her heart.

She wouldn't be able to dodge them this time. She was too slow, too in pain to react to their assault. Victory was his!

***

Why Justice? cried Ember. *Why must I fight this?*

Then quite unexpectedly, Ember found himself remembering Peace, kneeling before him, waiting to be destroyed. The scene played before his mind like a dream.

I owe him a debt...

Ember felt the comfort dragging him down, clouding his mind. He couldn't think. It was so comforting, so sweet, so smothering that it seemed almost unreal. He was lost in it.

Pain! Ember gasped. *I need pain!* It was the only thing that could cut through the fog. He needed Justice.

***

Deception felt time slow as they closed in on Glory. He kept his hand pressed against Ember's scales, feeding him the pleasure he craved. The final seconds seemed to blur. Highland was his!

***

Justice! I need you! cried out Ember. The pleasure was maddening. In it there was no right or wrong, no purpose, no ideals, no mission. Even to be in the wrong would be better if it meant purpose for life.

Justice, I beg of you—don't abandon me!

Then suddenly he felt a voice, whispering impossibly to him through the void.

Oh Ember. I never abandoned you. I never will.

Ember tensed, and then suddenly his body burned with fire!

***

Deception gave a cry and jerked his hand away; Ember's scales had suddenly become like blazing coals against his skin.

***

In a sudden flash Ember saw everything. The pain burned through the fog in his mind like a knife and suddenly he found that he could think again, that he could remember, that he could see! In one instant he saw that he was flying upward, in one instant he saw Glory right above him, in one instant he realized what was happening—what he was about to do—and his wings gave a painful jerk as he desperately threw himself to the side.

***

Justice leaped to his feet in elation when he felt the fire in Ember's mind, and when he saw his dragon go shooting out from beneath them, barely managing to avoid collision.

"He did it!" he cried with unmistakable joy. "He did it! He broke off!"

"Yes, he did," said the King smiling. "Just as I knew he would."

"Now I have to help him," said Justice quickly. "Deception is still there."

"Yes, you must," said the King. "But if you really do wish to save him, then there's something you should know."

***

Deception struggled with the rebellious dragon, trying to get him under control. "What are you doing?" he cried. He tried to send pleasure into Ember, but only burned his hand a second time on his scales. "Don't you realize he's going to kill you? That's the law! If you don't help me destroy him, then *you* will face the sword!"

Then I shall know that I died in the right, that I was where I belonged.

"You fool! Do you think you belong with that man? As if he needed you! He's Justice, the greatest swordsman in all of Tarenthia! He doesn't need a dragon to keep peace; his very reputation does that for him! You're nothing more than a pet to him! You're not needed!"

But I am loved—and I would much rather be loved than needed.

"Do you hear what you're saying?" cried Deception in rage. "Do you think this is normal of dragons? They've broken you! You should never have had this desire to be controlled!"

Then I count myself as blessed, for there is no better way of life.

"Better? How can it be better? It's completely unnatural!"

Then perhaps nature does not always know what is best. I choose purpose and belonging over freedom.

"What madness is this?!" cried Deception in disbelief. "Give up your freedom? And for what? Purpose? There is no such thing as purpose, Ember! Life is what we make it to be, and all that counts is how we choose to live each of our preciously short days. There is no meaning to life!"

That is not what I believe.

"You stupid creature!" cried Deception in rage, forcing his hand upon Ember's scales despite the pain. "I will teach you reason!"

Ember screeched as fire and pleasure clashed within him. Desperately he wanted to give up the pain, to let go of remorse and fall into comfort. He gasped. *Justice! I need you! I can't keep him out. I'll try to circle back...*

Desperately he forced himself to tilt in his flight, to return to the

King. He was losing vision now, his mind being pressed deep within him. He tried to hold onto the pain as he flew with all his might.

***

"Ember is coming back!" said Justice, making his way down Glory's back. "I'll have to jump to him. Will he fly under us?"

"Yes, Glory is adjusting our course so you will be lined up."

"Good! Then I will leap as he passes by. I'll have to be quick; I can't be more than a second off."

"Wait!" said the King. "What are you going to fight with? Do you hope to overcome Deception with your bare hands?"

Justice looked down and saw that he had indeed lost both of his weapons in the battle. Ember was approaching them now—it would only be a few more moments. He turned back to the King who held out his own sword.

"Take mine."

"The Sword of the Kings? But father, I am not..."

"You have earned it, my son. Take it and save your dragon."

Justice extended his hand and took the weapon. It was so heavy that he nearly dropped it. He struggled with both hands to hold it up.

"Many kings before us have wielded that sword," said his father. "This is the legacy of our kingdom; bear it well."

Justice nodded and turned back to watch the oncoming dragon. Any second now! He quickly moved to the edge, right next to Glory's beating wing, and braced himself. He counted slowly, bending his knees, gripping the sword. And then he jumped.

***

Deception lost his hold on Ember as he leapt up and spun around. There

was Justice, crouching between the dragon's wings and struggling to raise the Sword of the Kings.

"What are you doing here?" cried Deception, drawing his saber.

"I'm taking Ember back."

"I thought I got rid of you."

"I'm Justice. You can't get rid of me."

Deception growled. "Well, you're about to die right here, right now."

"I will kill you."

"With that sword? Ha! You're not worthy to wield it. See how heavy it is in your hands?"

Justice growled at him and Deception struck. Justice was immediately forced back as he could not bring the great sword up in time. Deception swung again and Justice managed a clumsy block, sending the clang of steel through the air. Again and again Deception slashed out with his sword, and again and again Justice was forced to retreat, his weapon too heavy to move at the speed he was used to.

Deception advanced upon him, pushing him to the edge of Ember's back, raising his saber high. Time seemed to slow as Justice cringed, trying with all his might to bring his blade up.

There wasn't enough time. Around him the world seemed to leap out in sharp detail. All at once he was aware of the rushing wind, of Ember's labored panting, of every beat of his wings, and of the blinding sun behind them. As if in a dream, Justice watched as Deception's saber came down and he strained every muscle, every fiber, to raise his own sword.

The blades collided just above his head with the ringing of steel, and suddenly the tip of Deception's sword was sent spinning off into the wind. The man looked at his weapon in horror, now several inches shorter, and Justice stared back in shock.

Then Justice laughed. Quickly, he made a swing of his own and Deception jumped back, fearful to block lest his blade be broken further.

Justice continued to advance and Deception desperately retreated, striking out when he could, but unable to counter the great sword's momentum. Again and again Justice lunged forward, and again and again Deception leapt back, until he found himself balancing on the edge of Ember's shoulder with nothing but empty space behind him. Then Justice brought his weapon down and Deception was forced to block it, his hand pressed against the flat of his saber, which bent under the weight.

Justice smiled as he bore down. "This looks familiar..." he said.

Deception growled as he struggled. "This is my dragon! I claimed him! He's mine!"

"He has chosen me, and no place is found for you here. You are defeated. And I cast you out!"

With a heave, Justice raised the mighty sword and brought it down with all his strength. There was a crash and then Deception was sent falling into the dizzying heights below, the pieces of his shattered saber spinning after him.

Justice fell back, breathing hard, and collapsed on Ember's shoulder. His grip on the sword weakened as he panted heavily. Beneath him Ember also panted as he struggled to keep level on the air currents, exhausted from his long, reckless flight.

Did we do it?

"Yes, we did it. He's gone."

I'm sorry, I'm so sorry...

"No, all is well. You came back, and that was a very brave thing for you to do."

Did I hurt Glory? asked Ember, wishing he couldn't feel the blood on the tips of his horns.

"Yes, you gave her two deep cuts, but she will recover."

I guess I deserve to die for my treason more than ever now.

"Ember," said Justice kindly, "you won't have to die."

What? I thought that the law said—

"I did too, but the King told me something I did not realize, or perhaps did not want to realize, before."

You found a loophole?

"It's not a loophole. Tell me Ember, do you view yourself as part of the Dragon Rider Pact and therefore bound to your Rider?"

Yes, of course.

"Then according to the law, your Rider is responsible for your actions. You are under his command and ultimately he, being the leader, answers for you both."

But I didn't listen to Peace. How can he bear my responsibility when I rebelled?

"Did Peace order you to kill him?"

Yes ...

"Then the blame goes to him."

But I left him! I was on my own for so long.

"Yes, but you are with me now and you have bound yourself to the Pact. Everything you have done is under its protection; Peace bears the blame for all you did until his death, and I for all you did thereafter."

But that means you will be guilty for my actions, for things you didn't do.

"Yes, I know. The village you attacked, the wounds you gave Glory, I will bear the guilt of both. Of course, you will still face punishment for disobeying your Rider, but you will not have to die for it."

Then what will happen to us both?

"Well, first we will both be punished and likely separated for a time. But the King has promised to be merciful; the two of us will soon be together again and we will reign as Rider and dragon over all Tarenthia, and then after that we will take up the crown."

As the two of them continued to fly over the battlefield, they looked down to see Deception's army fleeing before Highland's.

Justice smiled. "I'm glad you're on my side, Ember."

And I'm glad you're on mine. It wouldn't be so, had you not sought me out.

"You were worth it—you were worth it all. I love you my Ember, with all my heart."

And I you, with all my heart.

"My Eldar."

My Eldar.

Epilogue

The battle ended that day. It was no surprise to Justice or anyone else in Highland's army that the King was able to overcome the odds before him. Deception's army had been larger, but as they saw their dragons falling from the sky, and as Deception himself was killed and the King landed to lead his charge, many of the soldiers lost their courage and fled. They sought refuge in Sorrow's Pity and for the day they were safe, as the King still held to his promise to not attack before the full moon.

That evening Justice was pleased to see Guidance and his family making their way around the city to them, leading a host of fifteen dragons. Ember was especially joyful to see Fearful again and bounded out across the plain to meet him. At first Fearful did not recognize him because of his new color, but when he saw that he was indeed his friend, he ran out to meet him as well. Fearful was still a timid creature, and he tended to stay close by Guidance's side, but he had changed, becoming happier and more at peace. The other dragons seemed nervous in their new setting, but when they saw Ember speaking with Fearful, they began to approach him as well. They spent several days together in safety as the King set out to conquer the Shadowlands, and Ember especially enjoyed their company, as there had been no chance in his younger days to talk to other dragons his own age.

The forces of the Shadowlands did not sway the King. Even with his mount injured, they were still powerless to resist him. First, Sorrow's Pity was taken and then the other nations that had contributed to Deception's army. The only city to be spared was Despair, which had surrendered to Justice before the King had arrived. It took less than a week for the Shadowlands to be subdued and Deception's network to be destroyed. Afterward the King returned triumphantly, and the people of Highland held a great celebration unlike any before.

Several days were spent burying those on the battlefield, and during that time the broken body of Deception was found. He was buried without ceremony alongside his men, but not before Justice took back the Link he had stolen from Highland so long ago. He gave it to Ember, who had lost his own.

Soon, the time came for the King to leave the Shadowlands. Ember was greatly saddened to leave his fellow friends, although Justice promised that they would return from time to time, and that gave him comfort. On the day they were to leave, as the men of Tarenthia loaded the boats and as the rising sun glittered on the horizon, Justice took the chance to speak with Guidance one more time.

"Are you sure you have to go?' the old Dragon Trainer asked sadly. "I feel greatly unprepared to lead this country in your absence."

"I have no fear for you," said Justice kindly. "I can tell that you will guide these people and your dragons with wisdom. And besides, I'll be back in a few years to see how you're doing and to offer help if you need it."

"I thank you, Justice, for everything. You have done a great service for us and brought joy to so many of the creatures I have cared so long for. We can never repay you."

"You have no need to repay me. You were the one who chose to abandon Deception's force, and who led the others back here to the King. You will always be remembered for your bravery."

"Your kindness is unequaled," said Guidance bowing his head. Justice nodded in return. "Before you go," he said, holding out his hand. "I wanted you to know that I found this."

Justice looked and saw a Link, the one Deception had slashed from Ember in their flight during the battle.

"The chain is broken, but I believe that it will still work. I was wondering if I might be allowed to keep it, so that I could hear the thoughts of my dragons."

Justice looked at him, his eyes sad. "I'm afraid that is not within my authority to grant. Links are only given to Dragon Rider Pairs, and all this trouble was largely caused by one that had escaped that tradition. The Links were designed to create a bond between a Rider and dragon, and the bond would not be complete unless there was a Link for each of your dragons as well. I'm sorry, but this has to be returned to Highland."

Guidance nodded sadly and handed the chain over.

Justice eyed him. "Do not mourn, my good friend. You have been given much, and your responsibility is a special one that no one else has ever held. Lead your dragons such as they are, and do not desire a world that is not yours. Do the work you have been given, and when the time comes you will be rewarded accordingly."

Guidance nodded and smiled. "Very well, Dragon Rider. May your reign be peaceful. I look forward to seeing you again soon."

"As do I," said Justice as he turned to go. "May your reign be peaceful as well."

Shortly thereafter, he mounted Ember and flew out to join the departing ships, the dragon's wing having been permanently healed by the dragon trainer during the previous week. The other dragons followed them out over the water to see them off, and Guidance watched them go from atop Fearful, his own personal dragon.

***

Soon they all arrived back in Tarenthia, and the nations rejoiced to see the return of their King. Just as predicted, Justice was separated from Ember for a time, but before long they were flying out over the realm as Rider and dragon.

Shortly into their reign, the new king of Watergate requested a word with Justice, who came immediately. The young ruler apparently felt responsible for all that had happened, especially for Peace's death, and apologized profusely.

"I'm sorry," he said, "for all that we did, for everything Tyrant did. Our little squabble caused you so much pain and I wanted to make it up to you."

"There is no need," said Justice. "The conflict here may have set off our troubles, but you are not responsible for them. That was the fault of me, my brother, and Ember. The blame goes not to you."

"Even so," said the young king, "on behalf of my people, we wanted to offer you the emerald that we had all fought over."

He motioned behind him, and one of his servants moved forward bearing the emerald. He held it out to Justice, who spent several moments looking at it. The jewel was indeed beautiful, and its lovely shades of green shimmered and glowed with the refracted light that passed through it. Justice looked into the heart of the gem for several seconds, but then shook his head.

"No," he said. "This is your jewel; I would never take it from you. And besides, I have an emerald of my own that is far more precious to me." He bid the king farewell and turned to mount Ember, who had been waiting patiently.

And so for seven years, Justice and Ember kept the peace throughout the whole land. Some citizens thought that they ought to have gone on for ten years, as Justice had not already served three, but the King said it was unnecessary.

"The point of the Dragon Rider Pact is to develop a bond between the Rider and dragon," he had said, "and I believe that what Justice and Ember went through together in the Shadowlands was worth three years. Indeed, it is exactly that type of adventure I wish all Riders could go through if it were not for the higher risk of grave consequences."

And so together Justice and Ember kept peace among the kingdoms, and often it was said that never had there been a greater Rider pair than they. There were still times when Ember would remember something from the time gone by and be hit with a wave of longing, but he would hold fast through it until it passed by, and his Rider was always there for support.

On their missions he was the more cautious of the two, the one more likely to withhold judgment and to grant mercy, as he often could relate to those at fault. Justice was more stern than his dragon, and more prone to wrath, but he had also changed. He always dealt justly, but seemed less aggressive and tended to smile more often than he had before. Indeed, he had even developed such a sense of humor that he went through with his threat and dyed Ember several different colors during their first month ruling together. The nations that saw them mistakenly believed that Highland had somehow released four or five Riders at once, and such a fear came over them that there was neither talk nor whisper of war of any sort in that part of the country for nearly two years.

For the length of their time among the kingdoms, Justice and Ember kept peace throughout the land and had many great adventures together, although those are stories for another time.

The only other day worth mentioning was when they received their new names. It was a tradition for every Dragon Rider pair, after they had served their time, to return to Highland where in a great celebration the King would give each of them their new name that reflected who they had become, and then proceed to hand the crown over to the Rider and name him Highland's next ruler.

***

Ember stood before the King with Justice on his left and an enormous crowd behind. The ceremony was out in the courtyard of the castle, which was the only place where so many could gather, and the gentle rays of the morning sun warmed his scales. He looked up to the King before him, who was giving a speech to the crowd. To his left stood Glory, as black and magnificent as ever, and Ember quickly lowered his head.

What is the matter? he heard her ask. *You have no shame here.*

But Ember did not answer. Glory had healed fully from the day he had attacked her under Deception's influence, but somehow he still feared to be in her presence. As long as he had flown with Justice alone over the land of Tarenthia he had been happy. But now before the presence of the King and his dragon he suddenly felt a burden of guilt, as though he should not be there.

The King finished his speech, and the crowd cheered with a great cry. Slowly he strode over to Justice, who stood silent but smiling beside his dragon.

The King smiled back. "Are you ready, my son, to take the crown?" he asked, though softly so that no one else heard.

Justice gave his head a small nod. "I believe so, but I have wondered: was I right to defend Ember? I loved him with all my heart, I could not bear to see him die, but by denying my justice did I become unworthy for the throne, the place where the righteous rule?"

"My son," said the King with a smile. "We are all unworthy to rule. The authority we are given is a gift and a responsibility, not something we deserve. Yes, a king must know justice to command his subjects, but he must also know mercy."

"But did I not forsake justice in order to show mercy?"

"No, not at all; you only recognized your place. Why do you suppose that we enforce our laws? What right have we to force many nations to conform to a set of standards we have made up?"

"Because they are not made up, and they are not our own."

"That is correct. Some of our laws are our own making, but the majority are the same as those written on the hearts of everyone who is born—a law formed by a higher authority. You see, that is why we came to power. We saw around us nations that forsook that higher authority and the chaos it created. We prayed that we might be given the means to bring order, to act as messengers of the law and bring it to the nations. And so we were given the dragons."

"I thought we discovered how to tame them on our own."

"No, we did not have time for that. And we could not simply have experimented on eggs with live hatchlings. No, the secret was given to us through our prophets, and with it came the responsibility. We have to use that power to enforce one law and one alone, to act on behalf of our Creator to keep the nations at peace."

"Then would showing mercy be a failure to enforce those laws?"

"In a way, but that is not our job. We are to uphold the law, but a higher authority has formed it, and that authority will keep it. It is ultimately not with us where true justice resides. We, as mediators, are concerned only with how our actions may impact others. We forgive the wrongs done to us, and God deals with the wrongs done to him. For too long you have seen yourself as his enforcer rather than his messenger. You needed to learn to love, and now that you have, you are finally worthy to receive your new name."

Ember watched out of the corner of his eye as the King whispered a word in Justice's ear. He could have sensed it through the Link, but he made a point not to. Justice would tell him in his own time. But if he had to guess, something inside Ember told him that it would be "Comforter."

Then the King began to walk toward him. Ember immediately bowed his head and stared at the ground, afraid to look up. He heard the footsteps come nearer until they stopped right in front of him, but still he did not raise his head.

Ember, Ember; what is the matter?

It was the King.

Slowly Ember looked up into his eyes which were full of kindness. *I feel that I do not belong here. I am not worthy to rule with Justice after what I have done.*

Oh Ember, no dragon or man ever is. Even Justice is not without fault. You should have seen some of the trouble he got into when he was a child.

Ember smiled slightly. *But even still, I should not be here. Your son was killed because of me; I cannot possibly reign with Justice. What need of me has he anyway? I carried him throughout Tarenthia before, but now what use am I? He can rule on his own.*

Ember my friend, you don't understand. Tell me, why do you think dragons are allowed to stay with their Riders when they become King?

I am not sure. Surely not because they are needed.

You are correct. They are not needed anymore, but they still remain; they remain because their Rider wishes them to. Take Glory for example. She was not always named that, but when we had finished our reign as Rider and dragon she was given that name because that's what she was to me—she was my glory. That is the tradition for all dragons. Their Riders love them, and that is why they keep them close, even after they take the throne. You are cherished by Justice, and your new name will reflect that.

Did he take part in choosing it?

He had a suggestion, and I believe it to be good. Before you were called "Ember," because that is what you were when you were named. But now that term no longer fits you. The little ember that my son cherished grew into a flame, becoming brighter and stronger. But then it broke its bounds and became a destructive fire that burned and destroyed, to the point of even extinguishing itself. But then Justice found you and rekindled that ember, bringing life into you once again. And as you grew stronger with him, that fire burned within you and brought a pain that refined and hardened you, making you into something beautiful that only trials can create. Your new name will be "Emerald," for you are a precious gem sought after through much trial and adversity. May you ever be to your Rider as his greatest jewel.

And that is the story of Ember. There were many great Riders and Kings throughout Highland's history, and there are many great stories to tell. But if you ever go there and ask to hear their favorite tale, they will always tell this one: the story of their kingdom's greatest Rider, and of his Emerald.

www.ingramcontent.com/pod-product-compliance
Lightning Source LLC
Chambersburg PA
CBHW061216210726
48294CB00006B/1867